Fifty Shades of Black and White

Confessions of a Naughty Nun

by
Joan Fox

Strategic Book Publishing and Rights Co.

Strategic Book Publishing and Rights Co.
12620 FM 1960, Suite A4-507
Houston, TX 77065
www.sbpra.com

ISBN: 978-1-62516-615-9

Book Design: Suzanne Kelly

For my children
Megh and Tim

Acknowledgements

This book could not have been completed without the help and support of so many people. First, my family, Meghan, Quinn, Tim, Kelly, Addy, Bronwyn and Damien Connor. My readers, Bonnie Ryan, who read it twice, and Celia Baldwin who read the first run, offered many valuable suggestions, which I have tried to incorporate. My book club, the Retired Teachers of Mansfield, especially Bonnie, Shirlee, Lynn, Mary Francis, Joanne, Judy, Kate, Ellen and Harriet encouraged me at our monthly meetings. My Hampton Book Club, Maijo, Eunice, Mary, Jennifer, and Faith have listened to excerpts and laughed at the appropriate times. Michele Jordan gently nudged me when I needed it. My band of friends lived the story with me, at least part of it. My high school friends, Marge and Jane listened patiently to the stories over and over. And Nancy is reading it from above. She always believed I was a better person than I am.

Contents

What are religious vows?
Poverty
Chastity
Obedience
Nun of the above

CHAPTER ONE

The Postulant Year

I entered the Sisters of St. Edmund on September 8, 1959. I was 18 years old. My parents came with me to Holy Family Novitiate in Cumberland, Rhode Island along with my aunts and uncles and almost all my high school friends. Before Mom, Dad, and I left home, I said goodbye to my grandmother who lived with us at the time. That just about broke my heart. She was one of the most important people ever in my life.

Everyone stood around outside the novitiate talking and trying not to cry. I remember that it was a beautiful day, sunny and warm. Most of us wore colorful summer dresses and high-heeled shoes and even some pillbox hats. After all, Jackie Kennedy did influence our attire.

At two o'clock, Mother Christopher, Mistress of Novices, walked among the people ringing a bell and asking the prospective postulants to go in the convent and the families and friends to follow her into the chapel. Thirty-one young women ranging in age from seventeen to twenty-six went into the convent to change into postulant dress. The habits would come later. Our postulant outfit wasn't too bad. Of course, it was all black with a small veil attached to a cap. The dress fell to the ankles, gathered at the waist in wide pleats and had a loosely fitted bodice with long, narrow sleeves. Over the bodice was a detachable cape, which ended at the waist. This tied in the front at the neck under a white Peter Pan collar made of a kind of plastic. Matching white cuffs made of the same material slid over both wrists. I remember feeling pretty proud of myself. One of the best things about the postulant dress was the huge pocket. You could fit a picnic lunch for two in it. After placing us in order by age, we filed down to the chapel where there was a brief ceremony admitting us to the sisters of St. Edmund, or SSE's. My parents were shaken up when they saw me. My mother, who never cried, put her hand up to her eyes and brushed away a tear. My father paled; his expression was one of shock. I was their only child and here I was giving up any semblance of a normal life. The clothing we took off was returned to our parents in a bag. I can't imagine what all this must have been like for them.

The rest of the day was spent with family and friends and then we said our goodbyes. A final kiss and hug. I still remember my Dad whispering to me that he was proud of me but I could always come home. Then a final squeeze and I returned to the convent.

We called each group of entering postulants a band and seniority wise I was around the middle. Seniority was determined by age. Dorothy Mulvaney was two away from me in seniority and that meant she sat next to me for all meals in the refectory and in front of me in the chapel. This was really great because I knew her before we entered. We both had worked at J. J. Newberry's in Providence, Rhode Island. Alice Shanahan entered with us and she had worked at Newberry's too. Most of us had had part time jobs in high school to earn spending money. Alice was the second oldest in our band because she went to nursing school for a year before she entered. She had the ugliest red hair I ever saw. Her twin sisters, Meghan and Kelly, went to St. Pat's High with me and we had been friends since kindergarten. Meghan was a bridesmaid at my wedding. More about that later.

Our first night in the convent must not have been very traumatic because I don't remember much about it. We went to the refectory for our first meal in the convent. We stood quietly behind our small wooden benches and waited for grace to be said. While we waited, I looked at the food on the table. Lean pickings. There were platters of cold cuts, bread, and not much else. Water glasses. I thought, "If this is supper, what must lunch be?" I would be starved to death before the week was out. At home, most of us had our big meal in the evening because that's when Dad came home from work. In the convent it was the opposite, we had our big meal at lunchtime and a light supper in the evening. Thank God. So I didn't starve.

I was in St. Thomas's dorm along with about seven other postulants, organized by seniority again, and two senior novices. The senior novices were more or less in charge of us. One of them, Sister Mary Justine, was just too smiley. Nobody could be that happy all the time. The dorm consisted of eight "cells" formed by sheets hanging by hooks from pipes attached to the ceiling. When we entered our cells we drew the curtains together, providing a semblance of privacy. In our cells we each had a bed, bureau, and drying rack. We also shared part of a long closet along the wall in the dorm. At the end of the second floor hall, there was a huge dorm where about fifteen postulants shared space with an appropriate number of senior novices. The rest of us were scattered in other smaller dorms along the hall. Before dinner, we went to the chapel to chant the daily office. We postulants didn't participate because we had no clue what to do, but I remember being impressed with the rhythmic chanting. Since we were an active order, we did not get up in the middle of the night to recite prime, tierce, sext, and none. We chanted them before dinner each day. Contemplative orders get up at some ungodly hour in the middle of the night to pray the morning office. We were more fortunate since we "anticipated" the office hours. From the chapel we walked in single file by seniority to the refectory where we sat at really long tables, again by seniority. Grace was said before we ate and then we sat down and started to talk. Dorothy and I were thrilled to be next to each other, and, we had a great time meeting the other postulants. Little did we know that talking, at dinner or anywhere, would soon become a rare occurrence. At the head of our table was Sister Mary Kevin, the Mistress of Postulants. At the canonical novice table sat Mother Christopher, Mistress of Novices, and at the senior novice table sat Sister Mary Teresa, Assistant Mistress of Novices. These three women became very important in my life during the next few years. We immediately nicknamed them "The Big Three."

That evening after dinner, we had some free time to unpack and get settled in. Recreation began at seven and went till eight. Because it was so nice out, we walked up to the hill and the novices introduced themselves to us. All the time, "The Big Three" were observing our behavior and how well we began our adaptation process. Back to chapel at eight for evening prayers and then to our cells. There were a limited number of showers in the bathroom, so the lines were long. We hand washed underwear and stockings and hung them to dry on a rack in the dorm. Lights out at nine whether we were ready or not. After a while, quiet crying could be heard from postulants who were clearly homesick. Thus began our life as Sisters of St. Edmund.

How did I get here? All these years later, as I try to reconstruct my reasons for entering the convent, I am hard-pressed for an answer. I grew up in an active Catholic family. My father, Joseph, was born on August 23, 1905, in St. Patrick's Parish in Providence, Rhode Island, to Joseph Connor and Mary Sullivan Connor. He and his twin brother, Walter, had an older sister, Marie, who was very beautiful. A few years later William was born completing the family. When I was a little girl, my grandmother told me many funny stories of her children. She buried three of them in the influenza epidemic in the early twentieth century. My father was the only one to survive. He and his brother Walter were altar boys at Elmhurst Academy, a private Catholic School for girls near their home on Pinehurst Avenue. My Dad graduated from LaSalle Academy in 1923 and went on to Providence College, a Dominican school that was just down the street. At some point during that time, his father died and my Dad left college to support his mother, who was alone. He went to work at the Social Security Office in Providence where he met my mother, Irene Lebeau.

She was one of four children born to George Lebeau and Cecile Mullen Lebeau on January 2, 1914. Her family lived in many different places because her father worked on the Boston and Maine Railroad. Edward was born in New Market, New Hampshire, then my Mom in Charlestown, Massachusetts, Anita in Pawtucket, Rhode Island, and lastly, Agnes, born in

Providence. My mother attended public schools, graduating from Pawtucket Senior High School in 1932. From there she went to Rhode Island Hospital School of Nursing where she completed one year. She told me once that it was very difficult being a Catholic and a nursing student there. Attendance at Sunday Mass was required of Catholics under pain of mortal sin, yet the Catholic girls would be scheduled for work at that time. After leaving nursing school, she took a job at the Social Security Office and met my Dad. They were married at St. George's Church in Pawtucket, Rhode Island on June 3, 1939. I was born almost two years later on May 29, 1941.

I attended Catholic schools, went to church every Sunday and Holy Day of Obligation, and became imbued with Roman Catholic philosophy. In the fifties, Church and family greatly influenced who you were and what you would become. In high school, St. Patrick's in Providence, the religious life was touted as the highest calling for a young woman. We read the lives of the saints and learned how they were called by God to dedicate their lives to Him for the betterment of others. "Jesus said unto him, If thou wilt be perfect, go *and* sell that thou hast, and give to the poor, and thou shalt have treasure in heaven: and come *and* follow me." (Matthew 19:21) We were taught to "listen" for the voice of God calling us to religious life. I know I never "heard" the voice, but knew I wanted to do something worthwhile with my one life. Several of my friends were thinking of entering religious life and I'm sure that influenced me. Two years before, when I was a sophomore in high school, Mary Brennan entered the Faithful Companions of Jesus, a semi-cloistered religious order. Mary lived on the same street I did in St. Patrick's parish. She was two years ahead of me in school and was absolutely beautiful. Mary had two younger brothers, Bill and Frank. Bill was the same age as I and we dated in high school. He was a fabulous dancer. The Faithful Companions of Jesus had almost no contact with the outside world. They could write a letter to their parents twice a year and receive one from them twice a year. Mary's father was never the same after she entered. I thought she had made a very selfless, brave decision

5

about what to do with her life. I began to think maybe I could do the same thing. My best friend, Bonnie Ryan, planned on becoming a Maryknoll missionary after she finished nursing school. Maryknolls required post secondary education before they accepted you into the order. Again, I thought if she could do it, so could I. She eventually did join the missionary order and was stationed in a remote area of Venezuela. Once a month a bush pilot flew in with mail and supplies. Bonnie fell in love with him and eventually left the order but did not marry him. He was ready for marriage but she was not.

During my senior year of high school, I knew I had to make a decision about my future. According to the teachings of the Catholic Church there were three ways of life: religious life, marriage, and the single life. Supposedly, you were equally likely to be "called" to any one of them. I remember asking a priest at a retreat for high school seniors that year, "Suppose you were called to the married life and no one asked you? What then?" (Obviously, this was before feminist movement.) He said that he was sure that would not be a problem. I'm not sure if he was humoring me or avoiding a discussion.

A river starts somewhere up in the mountain, flows along, and meanders between rocks, over fallen trees with a few forks. The river doesn't decide where to go as the forks appear, but succumbs to forces outside itself for direction. Like the river at the forks I never did decide what to do, but flowed along like the river. It was all so long ago, it is hard for me to remember what I thought or felt. My recollection now is that I lacked courage to make a choice. I remember thinking that I wished my parents would say, "No, you can't go." I was hoping for an excuse. My grandfather told my mother, his daughter, not to let me go. She told me this but did not refuse permission. She didn't listen to him. Many years later I found out that her father had refused to let her go with a man she loved to Washington, D.C., where he was going to law school. Perhaps she regretted not going with him and so did not want me miss out on what she thought I wanted. My mother and I did not have heart to heart talks but we understood each other.

"Lord Jesus preserve us in Peace!" exclaimed the canonical novice who gave the wake up call the next morning at the ripe old time of 5:30 A.M. We replied "Amen" half-heartedly. I had never been up that early in my whole life! Even on our high school retreats we didn't get up till 7. And that was after being up all night talking and partying. I couldn't remember how to put on the postulant dress. Where were the hooks? Where were the mirrors? How could I check on how I looked? No mirrors in the convent, no mirrors at all. The ugly nun shoes, they were easy to put on, I could see what I was doing with them. Today, our first full day in the convent, we had to wear a corset, one with bones, if you can imagine. It was on the LIST of things we had to bring with us to the convent. We had to buy two, one in the wash and one to wear. I have no idea what the reason was for the corset, but there I was, putting on a white cotton undershirt and lacing up the corset over it. Once the dress was on, then came the cape and the veil. I picked up my missal and rosary beads and headed off to chapel. Sitting in the corset was no fun because the "bones" pushed up under our breasts and really hurt. A very helpful canonical novice told us to take out the bones and we would be fine.

On my way downstairs, I noticed a sign on the stair railing that read "Second Class." I wondered what that meant? Eventually I discovered that there were several kinds of days that related to silence. Every day we had two hours of recreation when we could talk, one in the afternoon and the other just before evening prayers. On a Silence Day, we did not talk at any meal. Third Class day meant that we could talk at dinner. Second Class allowed talking at lunch and dinner. First Class was the big buana of days because you could talk almost all day. Needless to say, these were extremely rare. Christmas was First Class, Easter, Mother Jordan's birthday (she founded the Sisters of St. Edmund), St. Edmund's Day, November 20, when the SSE's came to Rhode Island. And the day after Kennedy was elected President.

Of course, you could NEVER talk during the GRAND SILENCE. Grand Silence began after evening prayer and extended through breakfast, unless it was a First Class day. The morning chapel routine began with some short prayer and the mistress of novices banging her ring on the pew to signal the beginning of meditation. Think about that: I meditated for half an hour, every day. One could look at this with the half empty, half full mentality. Half empty - what am I going to meditate on? Half full - I don't have enough time to do all the meditation I want. My perspective vacillated between the two. On the positive side, I had time to really think about life: what's important, what's not, in a completely undistracted environment. At the end of the half hour, the ring banged the pew again and we began chanting the morning office: matins and lauds. Not too long before I entered, the office was chanted in Latin. That must have been tedious. Toward the end of chanting, the priest walked in for Mass. At that time, his back was to us as he said Mass and it was still in Latin. He never gave a sermon except on Sunday and some special holy days. For the next ten years, my day began pretty much the same way.

Silence played a huge role in my life as a nun. We kept silence in order to get closer to God. Silence freed us from interaction with others, so we could focus on our relationship with the Supreme Being. We strove to develop an interior silence as well as exterior silence. Walking through hallways we kept custody, which meant that we kept our eyes down; we didn't look directly at each other. We also walked close to the walls and away from the center of the corridors. And we kept our hands clasped under our capes: no sauntering for us. However, we did say, "Peace be with you" to whomever we encountered and that person responded, "and also with you." This was allowed even on Silence Days but not in the GRAND SILENCE. No one said anything during that time which extended from evening prayers to forever. Well, as I mentioned, it depended on what Class of day it was the next morning.

Fatima Sunday was a huge feast in those days. It commemorated the alleged appearance of the Blessed Virgin Mary to three children in Fatima, Portugal on six consecutive months starting on May 13, 1917, and ending on October 13, 1917. The novitiate made an annual pilgrimage on the second Sunday of October to the gorgeous shrine of Our Lady of Fatima which was right on the grounds, but down the hill and to the left, more or less in the public part of the novitiate. It was one of the visiting days for all the novices and postulants so you can imagine the number of people who came to this event. We used to come as high school students and try to make the young nuns look up. Because, of course, they had to keep their eyes down. Our mistress of postulants told us beforehand that we should keep custody and offer it up for a special intention and if we did, it would be granted. Well, the day arrived and we lined up for the march to the shrine. The postulants were followed by the canonical novices and senior novices in that order, all of us carrying lighted candles, which dripped down our hands all along the way. I think the big muck a mucks followed all of us. Their candles probably didn't drip. The road was lined with friends and relatives who were carefully looking for their loved ones. Of course, I peeked so I didn't get my special intention. At the shrine there was some kind of religious service, probably Benediction and a sermon. Afterward, everyone marched back up the hill and onto the recreation area in back of the novitiate. Then began the hunt for family. Oh, my God, it was so good to see everyone! Mom and Dad, especially. They looked well but Dad told me Nannie, my Grandmother, was not doing too well. I had the most visitors of everyone there. How vain is that. I actually counted! I think Jennifer Sheathelm had about the same as I did. My cousin Jerry was there with his fiancée, Rose. She asked me to take a walk with her, and I said no, because I didn't want to leave all my friends. I guess I never really liked her. I had the best time that day. It was almost like being home because so many people were there. But it ended and I went to chapel to prepare for the evening office. That night at recreation, everyone talked about the day and how wonderful it had been. We caught up on how everyone was doing and then headed back to chapel for evening prayers. In our dorm, lights went out and we all fell asleep. "Jimmy, stop, stop! Don't touch me there. Oh, that feels so good." Followed by giggling from Sister Nancy. She talked in her sleep and gave voice to our collective memories. This tended to happen after visiting days until Jimmy stopped visiting her. My last high school boyfriend couldn't visit me because he had entered the Christian Brothers. Oh, well.

The next morning, after breakfast was over, Sister Mary Kevin made an announcement. It would be our privilege to clean the wax from the Lady of Fatima Shrine. We all looked at each other thinking, "What?" We were given flat irons and newspapers and marched off down the hill to the shrine where, on our hands and knees, we put the brown paper bags on the spots of wax and ironed them off the flagstones. There was only one outlet at the shrine so we had to wait in line to reheat our irons. Can you imagine? Thirty-one of us on our hands and knees, melting wax. What were we thinking? I guess that's the point. We weren't thinking. We were probably imagining that we were humbling ourselves for the glory of God. Humility became very important to us.

Our days as postulants were filled with classes both religious and secular. Religious classes taught us about the rules of the community and the vows of poverty, chastity, and obedience that we would eventually take upon ourselves. Our other classes were equivalent to a first year college liberal arts curriculum: English, world history, French, and for me, calculus. We also were assigned charges otherwise known as chores. Some of us had kitchen duty, lavatories, hallways, parlors, etc. These were done right after breakfast and before classes started.

Sister Mary Scholastica was the superior of the whole novitiate, which included the professed side of the building, where the professed nuns lived and our side, where the novices and postulants lived. The professed nuns went out to teach every day at Blessed Sacrament, an elementary school run by the Sisters of St. Edmund. Sister Mary Scholastica was also the music director and loved to have the postulants and novices put on performances. This meant that we had to practice for these shows during recreation. Can you imagine, the one time we get to talk, and we have to practice singing? Well, she decided that we would do some of the songs from the "Sound of Music." Cute.

Anyway, I loved to sing! But I couldn't carry a tune to save my life. Now, in the convent, singing is considered praying twice, so it's really important. Here we are, in the huge classroom, sitting at desks, singing away, and she is going up and down the aisle listening for the parts. I was an alto and she was going back and forth beside me. Sister Mary Martha sat in back of me and she was really good: loud, too. But Scholastica couldn't figure out who was off. She finally realized it was I and asked me to lip sync the music. Can you believe that? I was asked to lip sync! So much for praying twice. (I had to lip sync in chapel too.)

Sister Mary Scholastica decided to put on an abbreviated version of "The Sound of Music." The first song of our performance was "How Do You Solve a Problem Like Maria?" And I actually did have a part in it. A fliberty gibbet, a will of the wisp, a clown. I said "a clown." I was a huge hit.

I'm trying to remember where we celebrated Christmas that year. It must have been in the recreation room just above the chapel. It was the senior novices' responsibility to decorate the recreation room for the Holy Day. When it was our turn as senior novices, we did it in red and green, Christmas colors. Sister Claire Marie in our band was in charge and she was a real artist. It looked fantastic. We had picked green pine boughs from the hill outside and put them everywhere, decorated with huge red bows. We didn't exchange gifts in the novitiate for several reasons. When to shop? No money; violated vow of poverty. Our families were allowed to give us gifts, but they were put into a pool and distributed according to need to whomever. That was harsh. I was so happy to see my Mom and Dad at Christmas. It wasn't on Christmas day, but probably the Sunday after. I missed being home and I missed all my family and the fun we always had together. On Christmas day my Dad and I usually visited my grandmother, Nannie, in the morning, often going to Church with her. I remember once when I was a little girl, I asked Santa for a boy doll and she got me one. It was my favorite present. I loved her and still feel so dearly her love for me. We had such great times together when I was growing up. My mother didn't get along with her at all – she was my father's mother. Whatever happened between them took place long before I came along. My grandmother never said anything bad about my mother but my mother badmouthed her all the time.

Mary Sullivan Connor, my grandmother, grew up in Providence, Rhode Island, and lived in the city her entire life. She married my grandfather, Joseph Connor, and bore four children. I have a sepia photo of the twins at about age 4 or 5, wearing long white dresses, white stockings, and black high button shoes. The picture is in its original frame; my grandmother probably put it in there and it stands on a bookshelf in my bedroom. I don't know which of the two is my father. William was the youngest. My grandmother used to tell me stories about them when they were small. All but my Dad died in the influenza epidemic in the early nineteen hundreds. I can't imagine what it must have been like for my dad to lose his sister and brothers. I wonder if he asked himself why did I survive? I am glad he did because he loved me, he loved me very much. People would tell me that his face would light up when I came into the room. He was the most important influence in my life.

Nannie lived in cubical shaped house on Pinehurst Avenue in Providence, Rhode Island. On the first floor there were 4 rooms; a reception hall as you entered through the front door, a parlor to your right, a dining room beyond the parlor, and a kitchen beyond the reception hall next to the dining room. The dining room had a pass-through to the pantry, which was off the kitchen. Nannie and I had so many good times in that house. I would sit on the window seat in the dining room next her on the rocker and we would talk about all kinds of things.

One of my saddest memories that postulant year was her death that spring. My Dad had come up to the novitiate to bring me something or other shortly after she died and for some reason I saw him as he was leaving. We waved to each other but I really wanted to go to him and hold him and cry with him because it was a love that was shared. How cruel of me not to have done that. It was a rule that we were not to have contact with our family outside of the permitted times. I see him still with his overcoat and bowler, arm raised in a hesitant wave. I miss him every day of my life.

Soon after we entered, we began college classes along with our religious training. I took calculus, French, world history, English composition, and philosophy. Our religious classes focused on the rules of our community and the Old Testament. Everything was going along pretty well and then

BAM!

We were introduced to Chapter. What, you may ask, is Chapter? How lucky you are if you have to ask. It's public humiliation, specifically designed to subjugate you, to instill a sense of humility. During chapter, you kneel in front of the mistress of postulants and the sisters in your band and publicly admit your transgressions of the past week. Now, we lived in the convent. How bad could you be? Usually, the transgressions were breaking silence, not keeping custody, failing to be in bed on time, having a particular friendship. I never admitted that, even though I loved Sister Mary Benjamin David. Not too many people admitted that although we all had particular friendships.

Sometimes the mistress of postulants gave a penance, such as a rosary, Our Fathers, Hail Marys, or ejaculations. In the Catholic Church, ejaculations were short, quick prayers such as "Jesus, Mary, and Joseph, have mercy on us." As students in Catholic Schools, we had created spiritual bouquets for our parents on holy days. The spiritual bouquet would have Masses, Rosaries, Our Fathers, Hail Marys and Ejaculations. We would fill in the numbers of each we would do for the occasion and present the card to Mom or Dad. I probably still "owe" some prayers. I think I once put down "5000 Ejaculations." That hasn't happened. Well, not the short, quick kind.

The summer before I entered the convent I went to see the movie "The Nun's Story" with Audrey Hepburn. I went with some friends who were entering the convent with me. In the movie, Audrey Hepburn participated in Chapter, but I NEVER thought the SSE's would ever do anything like that. WRONG. I also NEVER thought the SSE's would cut off your hair at

the Reception ceremony like they did in "The Nun's Story."
WRONG, again!

I signed up for the Sisters of St. Edmund in March of my
senior year in high school. It was quite a process. My parents
drove me up to the Novitiate. Once there, we met with the Mistress of Novices, Mother Mary Christopher, who helped us fill
out the appropriate paper work. Then she had some questions
and admonitions. First of all, I was to stop dating and therefore,
of course, could not attend the senior prom. (Jim and I were
going to mine at St. Pat's and his at LaSalle – the invitation of
the year in Providence.) And I was not to see "The Nun's Story."
Well, I went to both proms and saw "The Nun's Story." Obedience was never my strong point.

Evidently, just a short time before my band entered, the
SSE's used something called a "discipline." It was a strap with
small metal triangles glued to it and you hit yourself with it.
That would have been a deal breaker for me. I probably would
have been gone when that was presented to us. It's the same
thing the albino used in "The DaVinci Code." Some of the older
nuns still had their discipline in their trunks. I never saw one.

From time to time, a postulant or novice would leave the
novitiate. It was a very eerie experience. In the morning on the
way to chapel there would be a note taped to the railing in plain
view as we went downstairs. "Sister Ellen has left the novitiate.
Please keep her in your prayers." That was it. There was never
any discussion as to why, or when she decided, or anything.
Absolutely no discussion. Sometimes the note would appear in
the same place but at a different time, maybe after recreation.
I always thought it was so weird. There was so much mystery
surrounding the event. How did she get home? Did her family
come and pick her up? Did the SSE's call a cab? Why did she
decide to leave? It remained a mystery forever. We lost about
three postulants that year. One of them was really quiet and
pious. I was shocked when she left, but, looking back on it, I
think she was probably asked to leave. When I went to speak
to Mother Christopher about it, she said she thought I could
understand why she left. She had psychological problems. It

wasn't as much of a shock for a postulant to leave as it was for a novice - especially a second year novice - to leave. After all, they were almost professed, almost real nuns. So when one of their names went on the banister, I was pretty shaken up. What if I was wrong to stay?

One night during my postulant year I couldn't sleep. I was hungry. Really hungry. What would I do if I were at home, I wondered to myself – after all, this was supposed to be my home now. I would get up, go to the kitchen and get something to eat. Well, this was my new home, I thought, so I got up, descended two flights of stairs, walked along a very long, very dark corridor, past the laundry room, the altar bread room, the gunk room, (more about this later) the refectory, and into the kitchen. All this during the Grand Silence. At least I wasn't talking. Ah! Sunday buns. I lusted after the Sunday buns. Sister Mary Cabrini had them all laid out for breakfast. They were my favorite and to this day I have not found anything to match them. Just heavenly! So, I helped myself to about three or four of them, savoring every bite. Once satisfied, I returned to my cell on the second floor. I can still taste them.

So my little adventure constituted eating between meals, which was an infraction of the rule. This required humbly begging pardon and penance to Sister Mary Kevin, Mistress of Postulants. BUT, she was off somewhere so I had to go to Mother Christopher, Mistress of Novices. She had office hours and usually there was line of novices waiting in the recreation room, which was just outside her office. I got in line, looking totally out of place among the canonical novices. By the time I got in there I was a wreck. "Mother, I humbly beg pardon and penance for eating between meals."

When did you do this?
Last night.
What did you eat?
Sunday buns.
Sunday buns.
How did you get them?
I went down to the kitchen

In the pitch dark?

Yes, Mother.

(She's probably thinking what a nutcase.)

Say two rosaries and don't do it again.

The refectory, our dining room, – I use the term loosely – was long, narrow, colorless, and located in the basement of the novitiate. There was a series of small windows along the left side of the room as you entered. On the opposite wall hung pictures of various saints. Dominating the entire refectory was a likeness of Mother Jordan, our foundress, which hung on the front wall. At the end of the room were two smaller rooms with sinks where we could do the clean up. Most of the dishes and utensils were washed in the industrial sized dishwasher located in the kitchen. The kitchen was the domain of Sister Mary Cabrini. There was never any question about who was in charge there.

The postulants rotated responsibility for setting the tables and getting the food out before each meal. Those whose turn it was for refectory duty got to leave chapel early and go downstairs to put out the food. It was served on platters and placed on the three long tables.

After eating, each postulant and novice brought their dishes to the sinks at the back of the refectory, rinsed them off and placed them on a rack to be washed by the giant dishwasher. Canonical novices worked in the kitchen after meals doing the entire big cleanup, always under the watchful eye of Sister Mary Cabrini.

Every day we had to do some spiritual reading, usually the lives of the saints, and some other small book containing ideas for achieving spirituality. Actually, I think they were used for morning meditation aids. I'm trying to remember how and where we got the books for our reading. I don't remember a library anywhere in the novitiate. Sister Mary Kevin gave us the books; I guess based on what she knew of our spiritual lives – or lack thereof.

Toward the end of our postulant year, we were asked to write down three choices of names that we would like to receive. On Reception Day we received the name that would stay with us for the rest of our lives. In the Sisters of St. Edmund, it was the practice to be called Sister Mary "dah-dum." Mary, or some form of Mary, was in every Sisters of St. Edmund's name. However, at that time, there were so many nuns that they were running out of Sister Mary "dah-dum," so there was a possibility of becoming Sister "dah-dum" Mary. Our new name was a big topic of conversation at recreation. You could even be a double saint, for example, Sister Mary Benjamin David, my particular friend. So after much thought, I made up my mind. My first choice was Sister Mary Irene Joseph for both my parents, then Sister Mary Joseph Irene, and Sister Joseph Mary. Everyone waited patiently for the day of our Reception.

CHAPTER TWO

Canonical Novice

August 15, 1960, was Reception Day, our official entrance into the Sisters of St. Edmund. For the previous five days we were in retreat, total silence, prayer, and meditation focused on the step we were about to take. Reception Day began as usual with the office, meditation, and Mass. Afterward we had one last rehearsal, completed our charges, had lunch, and then returned to our cells to change into our best postulant's garb. Family and friends were invited and we would have a visit with them after the ceremony.

At the appointed hour, we marched into the chapel in our postulants' dresses and knelt in the prie dieu along the center aisle of the chapel. Prayers and hymns followed, with some words from the priest. At one point he turned to us and said, "What do you ask?" To which we responded, "We ask to enter the Sisters of St. Edmund." He blessed us, and then the postulants rose and marched out of the chapel. We went upstairs to our appointed places where a canonical novice then began to cut off our hair. Each one of us had already chosen a particular canonical novice to cut our hair. I chose Sister Mary Benjamin David. I remember her warm smile as I approached her and sat down. Taking a handful of hair in one hand and scissors in the other, she cut it off as close to the scalp as possible. This continued until almost all of the hair was gone. Then we took off our postulant dresses and, with the help of the novice, put on the habit of the Sisters of St. Edmund for the first time. The long black habit went on first, followed by the cincture and rosary around the waist. Next we put on the guimp and tied it at the back of our neck. On our head we put the white cotton cap with the starched forehead piece attached and tied it at the back of our head. It felt so uncomfortable. The canonical novice then pinned the white veil to the cap on either side of the forehead where soft fabric of the cap met the starched fabric. Our long, flowing sleeves were buttoned onto the habit at the shoulder under the guimp and we were ready. I felt beautiful.

Once again we lined up in seniority and marched back into the chapel. I cannot imagine what our parents must have felt as they watched their daughters coming in, dressed as nuns. For all intents and purposes, our lives were forever ended. Did we realize the magnitude of our decision?

I remember that during the second part of the reception ceremony, we had to prostrate ourselves on the floor with arms outstretched in the form of a cross symbolizing our death to the world. I remember that. I've never been in that position again. At least not on a hard wood floor… One by one, we approached the altar and the Bishop called each of us by our name for the last time and then gave us our religious name. To me, he said, "You will no longer be called Catherine Connor. You are Sister Mary Irene Joseph." Ideally, Catherine Connor no longer existed.

Following the ceremony, we met our families on the hill. Of course, the most important question they had was, "What name did you get?" When I said Sister Mary Irene Joseph, my parents actually cried. We hugged, holding each close. I think I got my first choice because I was an only child. There would be no grandchildren to carry on a family name.

After our reception into the order, we began our canonical year. All our classes this year were devoted to religious studies, no secular studies. We had classes in the rules of the religious life, the Old and New Testaments, theology. I really loved the biblical study classes because that's where I first learned of the apocryphal gospels. Saint Peter, one of Christ's apostles, wrote a gospel as did several other apostles - and from what I learned later - also Mary Magdalene. (I was not surprised by the references in the DaVinci Code.) Once again, one of the really big items that year was Particular Friendship. We weren't supposed to have any. So let me tell you about Sister Mary Benjamin David. She was beautiful, with the largest dark eyes I had ever seen and the kindest, sweetest disposition of anyone I had ever known. She was short with a slight limp because of a bout with polio when she was a child. We took to each other immediately. When I was a postulant she was a canonical novice. We always seemed to find each other at recreation, especially in the evenings when we would walk outside. When I didn't find her, my heart ached and so did hers. Because of the ban on Particular Friendships, we tried to fight our feelings, but it didn't work. I remember sitting opposite her one evening in the common room and our legs touched under the table and my stomach did a flop that I felt in my groin. I loved her. We loved each other. Our conversations were intimate, soft, warm, comforting. And we laughed together. She always thought some of the things I did were a riot. We never gave each other gifts and I was always measuring my feelings for her during our lectures on Particular Friendships, convincing myself that ours was not one because it didn't distract us for our search for God. Right. That was as close as I ever came to a lesbian relationship. I guess that's what the novice mistress was worried about. All those hormones and all those young women living together. I remember Mother Christopher at recreation with a flashlight and she would shine it in the faces of pairs of nuns walking together so they would separate. Chilling.

My charge (chore) during the canonical year was the altar bread room, another name for sweatshop extraordinaire. This is where the altar breads were made for the parishes throughout the diocese. There were nine machines. Numbers 1 through 8 made 6 large wafers and mine, number 9, made twelve. It was a huge waffle iron with 12 circular discs engraved with religious symbols. It was my machine and here is how it worked: I carefully poured the batter on the surface of the machine. Then I grabbed the handle on the lid with both hands, put all my weight on, pulled it down, and locked it shut. Meanwhile the sweat was pouring off my face. I then scraped the edges of the machine and put the gunk (scrapings) into a bowl, (they started to smell after a few minutes) and after the batter cooked for just the right amount of time, I pulled up the lid. (While it was cooking, the novice mistress urged to say ejaculations, commune with God.) Hopefully, the sheet would be perfect and not burnt or under-cooked and sticky. Because it was all for God, the sheets had to be perfect. Mother Christopher checked them occasionally and could be a real pain. Sister Mary Simon, another canonical novice in my band, mixed the batter. That was not such a hard job, but she had to get the right consistency. If the batter were too thin, the sheets would burn. It was also her responsibility to pour it into our bowls so we could pour it on the waffle iron. While we worked there, of course, there was no talking. And we kept custody so we could pray silently. (I'm thinking it's so hot I can't pray.) I have never been that hot, not even in Jackson, Mississippi, in the middle of summer. The sheets of hosts were stacked and given over to the cutters.

Sister Mary Benjamin David was a cutter. That was a tricky job. First, you had to cut out the large hosts, the ones for the priest to use at the elevation in Mass, and then cut the small hosts. You had to be careful not to chip the edges because they couldn't be used for the Body of Christ. The thought that these waffle irons were producing wafers that would become the Body of Christ was to be meditated on while we sweat. Back to the gunk for a minute. We had a gunk room where we dumped the filled bowls every so often in the morning. The gunk room had large metal garbage cans with covers and the room smelled awful. I don't know what happened to the gunk from there.

After lunch the canonical novices went to the sewing rooms, either black or white. Sister Mary Baptist was in charge of the black sewing room, and she was tough. We had to make the postulant dresses for the incoming band.

Later in the afternoon, after recreation, all the novices and postulants had to fill their altar bread orders. Each one of us had a parish to do. If your parish was small, then you had two parishes to do. This preparation included counting the large and small hosts, packing them in boxes in tissue paper, tying and addressing them to be mailed to the parishes.

If you did not have the altar bread room as a morning charge, then you had laundry. I never had laundry. I sweat. In the laundry, they had a huge mangle for ironing sheets. They had washers, gigantic washers, but no dryers. Everything was hung outside to dry whether it was January or June. A charge in the laundry was to go out every day just before supper and tighten all the clotheslines so they would be ready for the next day's wash. One day in early spring, Sister Mary Nora, my friend Alice Shanahan from Newberry's, whose responsibility was line tightening, looked outside at the pouring rain, almost like a hurricane, and decided not to go out to tighten the lines. After all, who would expect her to get soaking wet? Big mistake. When it was time the next morning, to hangout the laundry, the clotheslines were just about on the ground. Sister Mary Teresa, assistant mistress of novices, was furious and Sister Mary Nora was in so much trouble. She thought she was going to be sent home.

The laundry charge also entailed folding and delivering laundry to the nuns' cells. I think this was probably pretty cool because you could see how their places looked. Talk about "Design on a Dime." Actually, they all looked exactly the same.

Some of the high muck a mucks had parlors for a charge. What a joke. They had to mop and dust. Did they sweat? No. But it was the first place Mother Christopher saw when she left the chapel after breakfast to start her day. If she saw a speck of dust, you had to do the whole room over. Ouch. That was really harsh. The parlors were where we met our visitors. And of course, there were bathrooms to clean. Sister Katherine Mary didn't mind that charge because she said that her hands were always in clean water. Depending on the size of the bathroom, there would be one or two novices assigned. I never had the bathrooms as a charge. I pretty much spent my canonical year in the sweatshop. And some of the novices had offices to clean, like that of the Superior, Sister Mary Scholastica, the Mistress of Postulants or the Mistress of Novices. I'm glad I didn't have them.

As canonical novices, we were really secluded. We saw our parents only four times that year: at our reception in August, then on Fatima Sunday in October, on Christmas and on Easter. All the talk on Fatima Sunday was of the election, Kennedy vs. Nixon. Guess whom we were supporting? It was 1960 and a Catholic was running for President. There was electricity in the air: we all felt it. Of course, we saw no newspapers and definitely no television. But any of us who could vote – senior novices - were taken to the polls that Tuesday in November. The next day, there was a note on the banister. "John F. Kennedy is the new President. Please keep him in your prayers. First Class." We were ecstatic! As we passed each other on the way to hang out our laundry, we smiled openly! No custody that day. Even Mother Christopher seemed really happy.

The trunk cellar was located in the dark, musty, basement of the novitiate, just below the chapel. The trunks were on risers so they wouldn't get wet in case of flooding. There were about three rows of trunks on each side and the rows were long, extending from the door at the end of the hall to the exit door to the outside. We were allowed to go to our trunks once a month on a Sunday afternoon to get something or put something in it. I always liked going to my trunk because it reminded me of home. That's where I packed it with my Mom and Dad. We filled it with items on our list. I remember having extra underwear in there - in case you're wondering, it was not from Frederick's of Hollywood, more like what's advertised in AARP magazine - and school supplies. I also had a black winter shawl and boots and an umbrella. Because of our vow of poverty, we weren't allowed to have much. And that was okay with me. But I did love to muck around in my trunk. Sister Mary Walter's father made it. She was my sponsor. For a professed nun it was a big deal to have someone enter "under" you. Some professed nuns had seven or eight that entered "under" them. I guess if you taught high school, you had access to more young people who might want to enter.

On warm summer evenings we had supper on the hill. It was such a welcome respite from our routine. The canonical novices arrived with our hot dogs, rolls, ketchup, mustard, pasta salad, tossed salad, cold drinks, and chocolate chip cookies. We sat

23

on the grass, talking and laughing. I still have warm feelings remembering those times.

Mother Christopher was the Mistress of Novices and one of the few truly holy women I met in the convent. I thought she had a direct line to God. She prayed with her whole body and seemed to be in another world. She was tall and a little overbearing to us novices. When she was angry with us, she rose up a few more feet and became the angry black giant. During chapter she was impossible to figure out. You never knew if she would rake you over the coals or go easy on you. And it didn't seem to matter what the transgression was, but more what she thought of your "State of Grace" – or lack thereof. And she knew, oh she knew. It was uncanny. Of course, she was as Irish as Paddy's pig. Her name was Michele Jordan before she became a nun. Her family ran a funeral home in South Providence. Some forty years later, long after I left the convent, I went to visit her at the novitiate and sadly found that she had died just two weeks previously. I would have loved to see her and talk to her, tell her about my life. I always had the feeling that she liked me, in spite of all my failings. I think I made her laugh.

Another time I was really upset because a member of our band left shortly after our reception and I had thought she was so holy compared to me, for sure. So I went to talk to Mother Christopher about it. I waited in line outside her office and upon entering, knelt down and told her that I was devastated about Sister Mary Mark leaving. She said to me that surely I could see Sister Mary Mark was not suited to religious life. Actually, no I could not see that. But Mother explained it all to me so that by the time I left, I was okay and even felt that she thought there was hope for my religious life.

As canonical novices we were still in the old chapel. We sat according to seniority and so I ended up in the first seat in last row of seats by the windows. Now with all those women in there praying it can get a little gamey after an hour or so. Of course, we weren't allowed to use tampons, only Kotex and not the real Kotex, some other cheap brand. It was my job to get up and open all the windows with a very long pole to air out the chapel just before the priest came in to say Mass. After all, we didn't want him fainting with the odor. So I did this every morning at the beginning of the third office hour. Now I want you to think of a Gregorian chant CD and get into the mood of calmness and peace that it evokes in you as you listen to it. That's what we had every morning. It was beautiful. The sun was shining through the windows. Now, I am not a morning person, so half the time Sister Rita Mary, who sat in back of me, had to nudge me to remind me to get up and open the windows. So this particular morning, I forgot to get up so she nudged me. Okay, okay. I got up, bent over, grabbed the pole and lifted it with gusto because I was mad. It accidentally hit against the metal radiators and it crashed to the floor causing the entire chapel to fall silent. Chanting stopped and there was this terrible moment where I thought my breath sounded like a tornado. After some moments of total silence, Mother Christopher alone started up the chanting again. Oh, my God, I thought I would die!

Of course that resulted in major punishment for me. Not only did I have to publicly apologize in chapter for what I did, but I also had to beg pardon and penance from Sister Mary Scholastica, the superior of THE WHOLE CONVENT. I was terrified. Oh, my God. I had to go to her office on the professed side of the building, sort of like crossing the Berlin Wall. It was awful. Sister Mary Scholastica was okay, though. Now, as I look back, I think I remember a smile trying to be hidden.

Once a year the entire novitiate went to The Villa, a huge Victorian mansion on the ocean in Massachusetts. Right after breakfast, we boarded buses that would take us to the beach. Of course, there was silence on the bus so that we could get our prayers and spiritual reading in before we arrived. Once we got there, we went upstairs to change into our "beachwear." We were not allowed to wear bathing suits, but instead, wore our gym suits from high school. On our baldheads, we wore bathing caps. Otherwise, it would have been really gross. So into the water we went and stayed there all day. After all, it was a once in a year chance. Needless to say, we burned to a brilliant red-orange and could barely walk for a week. Kneeling was so painful. The postulants and novices had only one day a year there, but, once we took our vows, we could stay for a week.

Another responsibility of canonical novices was to read aloud during silence meals, not breakfast, just lunch and dinner. Some of us were better readers than others so the better readers did it more often. I was a pretty good reader so I did it a lot. When you were the designated reader, you read aloud while everyone was eating in silence. A second designated reader would eat her meal rapidly so she could relieve the main reader. It got to be a kind of competition to see who could finish eating first to do the relieving. The reader sat between Mother Christopher and Sister Mary Kevin in the front of the refectory at a student chair, one with an armrest. Mother Christopher would give the high sign to stop when she saw that everyone had finished their meal. Then the entire assemblage would rise and give thanks for the meal and file out in silence.

We all sat by seniority at the tables in the refectory but we rotated to the head of the table each week. And we rotated in groups of four, two on each side so Mother Christopher could get to study us more closely. Mother Christopher had a more substantial breakfast than the rest of us. It included a soft-boiled egg in an eggcup. Well, one morning Sister John Mary, Sister Rita Mary, Sister Thomas Mary, and I were at the head of the table. Mother Christopher had not shown up for breakfast yet and it was almost time to leave. Not wanting to waste the egg, Sister John Mary ate it. Oh, my God, we couldn't believe she did it. Not thirty seconds later – the egg still warming her insides – Mother Christopher showed up. No egg. She didn't bat an eye and ate her breakfast in silence. From that point on, we didn't touch her egg.

Sister Mary Ann was just a few seats down from Sister John Mary and me. She had a terrible time with the guimp. As I mentioned before, it was made of some highly flammable material and was easily cracked. We actually had two guimps, one for every day and one for visitors. Well, Sister Mary Ann cracked her guimp so often, that Mother Christopher made her wear linen one. It had to be starched and was impossible to keep clean. Sister Mary Ann had a terrible time with it and obviously stood out among us because her guimp was linen. Well, it got to be a few days before visiting day, a rare occasion for canonical novices, and Sister Mary Ann did not want to meet her parents wearing the linen guimp. What would she say to her family? What would they think? Everyone else had the normal guimp. So, she asked Mother Christopher if she could have a regular guimp for visiting day and Mother Christopher agreed. She probably didn't want to answer any questions from Sister Mary Ann's parents, either.

Our canonical year came to an end in the middle of August. We looked forward to becoming senior novices and starting the final preparation for our first vows.

CHAPTER THREE

Second Year Novice

As a second year novice I found myself to be a changed person. I was much quieter, more introspective, more detached. It was what I thought I should be, a far cry from my fun-filled postulant days. The intervening canonical year had done to me what it was supposed to, separate me from all I held dear. Lose myself in God. I definitely lost myself, forgot Catherine Connor.

We began our preparation for first vows with more classes on religious life and especially on the vows of poverty, chastity, and obedience. Poverty meant that we would have nothing of our own. We had to give away all our worldly goods. Actually, we signed a will leaving anything that might be ours to the Sisters of St. Edmund. Poverty of spirit meant that we detached ourselves from our family and friends, a continual struggle. Chastity is fairly self-evident. No sex. But we learned that it also meant developing a love of Christ since, once we took our vows, we would become Brides of Christ, promising to remain chaste and faithful to Him for the rest of our lives. Obedience required total resignation of our wills to the will of God, made known to us through rules and the directives of our superiors, namely Mother Christopher. We had to rid ourselves of pride and submit our wills to God.

Along with these religious classes, we resumed our college courses. I took classes in calculus, history, English, and philosophy. My favorite class was a philosophy course, ontology, the study of essences. I still want to learn more about it.

Our days were filled with charges, classes, prayers, etc. Believe it or not, my charge that year, at least for a while, was parlors A and B, located just outside the chapel. Bad luck for me because every morning as Mother Christopher left chapel after her morning prayers, the first thing she saw was my parlor. And she always found it lacking in cleanliness. Unbelievable. She could find a speck of dust on the head of a pin, so you can imagine what she found in my parlor. And the floors had to be polished every week with an industrial-sized floor polisher. The polisher literally dragged me around the room, reminded me of the #9 machine in the altar bread room, invariably hitting the legs of the tables and nearly knocking down the lamps. And the buffing had to be done in a specific pattern, resembling tangent arcs, overlapping, from one side of the room to the other. Now, you have to understand that these parlors were used ONCE A MONTH, for visiting day and yet they had to be immaculate all the time. Yikes, it was frustrating.

Another charge I had that year was the provincial house where the leaders of the community lived. It was located up the hill from the novitiate and a group of us had to walk up there every morning to clean. That place never got dirty either. Mother Mary Alban was the Provincial at the time and she was as broad as she was tall. And she was a gardener. She grew geraniums, which had to be watered, and watered in a timely manner. Well, that was my charge and I was not so good at it. Mother Alban gave me a private lesson on watering the damn geraniums. And they had to be picked, the dead stuff taken off. I didn't have that charge very long.

Sister Carol Mary and Sister Marie Claire, both members of my band, had kitchen duty for a charge early that year as senior novices. One of their responsibilities was to prepare the vegetables for dinner. In the morning before classes, they peeled potatoes and carrots, chopped, sliced etc. Then, after morning classes, they returned to the kitchen to mash potatoes and what-ever else Sister Mary Cabrini wanted them to do. One day they were a little late and so were rushing to get the potatoes mashed in the huge machine. The beater rotated furiously and Carol scraped the sides with a wooden spoon to make sure everything was mashed. The spoon got caught in the beater and splintered up into the potatoes. The fear of God and of Mother Christopher prohibited her from telling anyone, so we all ate the potatoes. A recent chest x-ray of mine showed a small tree growing in my large intestine. I know where this came from…

The really pious novices got the chapel for a charge. I never had the chapel for a charge. I had the sweatshop (the altar bread room), parlors, kitchen duty, geraniums, basement corridor, (that was a killer because the burner was there and I had throw all the stuff in the burner). When the scraps from the old guimps – especially from Sister Mary Ann - were tossed in the burner, they literally exploded. We heard tales of nuns who had been disfigured by fire when their bib caught the flame of a candle. I don't know if the stories were true but they were effective because we were very careful around the burner.

In the novitiate, we had two sewing rooms, the black sewing room and the white sewing room. In the black sewing room we made our habits, the "dress," sleeves and yoke. In the white sewing room, we made the coifs, our cotton head coverings and the large white veils. The white sewing room was especially fine work whereas the black sewing was more forgiving. Even so, the black sewing room became a source of consternation to me. Every year, we had to redo our habits. Wait till you hear this. This is what we did: during our postulant year, we made our first habits in an afternoon sewing class. We made two, one for everyday and one for special occasions. During the summer of our canonical year, we took apart our everyday habit, turned it upside down, and remade it into a "new" every day habit. In other words, the part that trailed on the ground during our postulant year now was gathered at the yoke on our breasts and what was gathered at the yoke last year was now falling by our feet. Nuns may very well have been the first recyclers. We also wore underarm shields to absorb the perspiration. These were washed out every night and hung on our drying racks in our cells. I'm not sure what happened to our good habits.

It was our turn to decorate for Christmas! The old chapel had now become our recreation room. Sister Claire Marie, our artist, decided to do all red and green and we were the first group to decorate the old chapel for the holidays. We had so much fun doing it. Everything was secret until Christmas morning. We collected live greens from the hill and formed them into garlands and wreaths decorated with red bows. The tables were covered with red and green cloths and adorned with white candles. By the time we finished, it was magnificent. Everyone really loved it. The doors opened on Christmas morning to oohs and aahs and huge smiles. It was especially gratifying to see the looks on the postulants' faces; their first Christmas away from family might not be so bad after all.

Winter months dragged along, highlighted only by Lent. That should give you some idea of our "good times." Lent was a highlight, day after day of prayer, fasting, and yet more silence. We had already given up so much just by entering the convent that it was hard to think of something else to give up for this penitential season of forty days and forty nights. There was more silence than ever; gloom and doom prevailed. Thank God for St. Patrick and St. Joseph, two feast days that brightened up our Lenten days. Holy week began with Palm Sunday and ended with Easter. The Catholic Church really gets into the rituals of Spy Wednesday, Holy Thursday, and Good Friday. We were in the chapel a lot that week.

As senior novices, our visiting days with family and friends returned to once a month. Now that I had been gone from home for two years, the number of visitors declined and it was just my Mom and Dad who came on a regular basis. This was okay with me because it provided me with an opportunity to talk with them, see how they were doing. And how the family was doing. They never complained about my decision to become a nun, to basically leave them and follow such an unnatural path. I am grateful to them to this day for their unquestioning support.

In August, we began our retreat to prepare for first vows of poverty, chastity, and obedience. The retreat followed the rules of St. Ignatius. Jesuits led it: all hell, fire, and brimstone. I can't stand the Jesuits. They are so arrogant, so self-important. I can't remember how many of us took our first vows. The only part of the ceremony I remember was prostrating ourselves again, this time on a marble floor. We must have left the chapel at some point to remove our white veils and don our black. Now we looked like real nuns. At some point during the ceremony we pledged our simple vows for three years. Afterward, we had a visit with family and friends. My parents, aunts, uncles and cousins came for the ceremony. This all took place on August 16, 1962, in Cumberland, Rhode Island. Our novitiate days were over. We were off to The Villa for a week of sun and sand and relaxation before we moved on to the Juniorate.

CHAPTER FOUR

Juniorate

Fresh out of the novitiate, wearing our new black veils, we headed for the Juniorate located in East Providence at St. Anselm's, a K-12 Catholic school for girls. It was once a boarding school and so had lots of room for us. The purpose of the two year juniorate was to continue our religious formation and complete our college degrees.

My parents were happy that I was at St. Anselm's because it was closer to Providence and I got to see them more regularly. Not only that, but we nuns could actually go out into "the world." My parents could drive me and my partner to visit family or friends who were ill but we could not have anything to eat or drink while we visited. Whenever we left the juniorate, we had to have a "partner" with us. I'm not sure exactly why. Maybe it was to prevent any sinful behavior. As you'll see later in my religious life, it wasn't effective, at least not for me.

The building where we lived at St. Anslem's was a cube and, at each corner, there were these huge rooms that housed about six or seven juniors. There were windows on two sides and beds arranged much the same way they were in the novitiate. Once again, curtains separated our cells from each other. Some juniors had double or triple rooms along the hallways, which connected the four corners.

One of these rooms was a single and that was for Sister Mary Stella, the Mistress of Juniors. I could not stand her. She had this perpetual smile on face that made me just want to slap it. Even when she was calling us on the carpet for something, she had this insipid smile. And raised eyebrows, permanently raised. She was light complexioned, tall, nice shape, at least what you could discern under the habit. She was very tall, although not as tall as Sister Mary Scholastica, the choir director. She never looked at you when she talked to you. I didn't like her. And she didn't like me. So that worked out. We more or less avoided each other. God, she drove me nuts. It was that perpetual smile and the feeling I got that there was no substance to the woman. I did not like the juniorate that much. And I was sick a lot while I was there. Nothing serious, just always sick.

It was Sister Mary Stella's responsibility to conduct Chapter for the juniors and to hold classes on the religious life. She was supposed to prepare us for life on the missions. The missions were local parishes where we would be sent after we graduated from college and could take our places as teachers in the parochial schools. Two of us were nurses and two were on a business track, but the rest of us were classroom teachers.

A regular day at the juniorate began with chapel, office, Mass, breakfast, and getting on the bus for Salve Regina College in Newport. The chapel was dark, with lots of brown wood on the walls and floors, stained glass windows high above the stalls on either side of the chapel. Even the chandeliers were dark. Along each side of the chapel were stalls where the youngest nuns prayed and then there were about twenty pews on each side of the center aisle in back of the stalls. The dreary altar faced the congregation of nuns. The sacristy was off to the right of the altar. I sat in a stall on the left side of the chapel. I can't remember where Stella sat. God, I did not like her.

The entire time I was in the novitiate, I never had the chapel as a charge. Finally, at St. Anselm's I got it. The only thing I remember about it, though, is that I caught a bat in the sacristy. One evening before prayers, I went in to put some freshly ironed albs in the closet. (An alb is the long, white linen gown a priest wears under the chasuble.) I turned on the light, and there, hanging from the crown molding, was a bat. Now, I am terrified of bats, but I knew I had to get rid of it before someone got bit. (We didn't have to worry about the hair thing.) So I grabbed a towel, folded it over, climbed up on the counter, stood up, reached out and grabbed the bat in the towel. I jumped off the counter, ran out of the sacristy, through the chapel, into the corridor, down the stairs to the burner. (It was similar to the one in the novitiate.) I opened it and threw the bat, towel and all into the burner. Then I collapsed on the basement corridor floor. Oh, my God! I had felt it move in my hand while I ran to the burner. Eventually, I got up and went back to chapel.

We had the most fantastic cook, Al, who was a joy to work for. He was a real gem. I can still see him running around the kitchen with a real white chefs hat and huge pots in his hands, juggling them and utensils and vegetables for the soups. He was a great cook. And he cared about all of us. Although he did have his favorites, Sister Mary Stella was not one of them! When her back was to him, he would mimic her mannerisms perfectly while we tried so hard not laugh.

The refectory in the juniorate was a huge room filled with about seven long tables, and about thirty nuns sat at each one, organized again by seniority. The finally professed nuns sat closest to the kitchen door, next the second year juniors and lastly, us, the first year juniors. As luck would have it, Sister Mary Scholastica was transferred from the novitiate to Bay View, so still no singing for me.

At the head table was a collection of unique, primarily VERY senior nuns. It was our first experience with senior nuns, after having been cloistered in the novitiate for the last three years. Sister Mary Margaret, we called her clean Maggie, provided us with much amusement. She was a classic case of obsessive-compulsive behavior. Every meal, she brought her own flatware wrapped in a clean cloth napkin to the table. Food was served family style. In the kitchen, Sister John Mary dropped a chicken on the floor, quickly picked it up – five-second rule – put it back on a platter and placed it in front of clean Maggie. If she only knew…

Then there was Sister Mary Agatha, Aggie, about a hundred years old and a rocker - not musically - back and forth in her chair near the Superior. Aggie was also inclined to speak loudly and say what was on her mind, definitely disconcerting for the

Superior who never knew what would come out of her mouth. "Damn Al. Where are my eggs?" We would be in hysterics down at the end of the table. She was something else.

Every morning after breakfast, the juniors who went to Salve's campus in Newport boarded a bus for the ride to classes. On the bus we could do our spiritual reading, finish our office, or study. Silence was always observed. I loved looking out the window at the "world" which I had not had the opportunity to observe for three years. Imagine! I hadn't seen anything beyond the convent walls for three years.

That's probably one of the reasons why college life for me was so great; such as it was for nuns, radically different from most peoples' experiences. There were four math majors at Salve in 1962: Sister Mary James Patrick, Sister Mary Simon, Arlene Becker–a regular girl – and I. What a kick Arlene was. The other girls at Salve gave her a hard time because she had most of her classes with three nuns. I loved it. Every Monday she would fill us in on her weekend experiences with her two boyfriends. I remember one of them already wore a "rug" and she made him promise that he would never take it off in public and the other one ran the Boston marathon. She married the one with the rug. She also became a math teacher like the three of us.

Math classes challenged us quite a bit, mostly because we didn't have much time to study. But I guess not many students studied because they partied a lot. They partied, we prayed. One of my first classes at Salve was the history of math taught by Sister Mary Bertha. She was one mean nun, really mean. She never smiled and got furious with the four of us for any and every little thing. I did love the history of math, though. Sister Mary Bertha had us fill out file cards on famous mathematicians with specific information about each one. I really enjoyed this assignment because it put into perspective how mathematics developed over the centuries. We also had a project to complete on a topic of our choice from the history of math. I chose to do the Newton - Leibnitz controversy about the discovery of calculus. I loved researching this and wrote a fairly good summary of my work. Sister Mary Bertha was not impressed. So as my final project I did a time line of the history of math and asked Sister Carol Mary to illustrate it for me. It was a work of art and I thought, of great substance. Sister Mary Bertha was still not impressed.

My favorite topics in that class were the three unsolved problems of ancient mathematics: squaring the circle, trisecting an angle with straightedge and compass and doubling the cube. I was fascinated by the mathematics that was discovered throughout the centuries while trying to solve them.

Anyway, as seniors we had a lay teacher, Miss Harrigan, an honest to God old maid. I can still see her teaching the four of us. She would come into the classroom, wearing brown tie shoes, a dark printed dress with a high, white collar, long sleeves with white cuffs, short frizzy hair parted in the middle and no makeup. She would turn to the board, say "Theorem, proof," write them out, facing the board. We'd copy them into our notebooks and then she would erase the board beginning at the top left of the board across to the right and then back to the left until the board was clean. Then she would start all over, "theorem, proof." I thought I would go out of my mind. I couldn't stand it. I wanted to slap her up the side of the head, I wanted to shake her, and I wanted to make her alive. I had her for probability, linear algebra, and senior seminar.

In senior seminar, I wrote a paper on rings and ideals. Sound romantic? They're algebraic structures. While writing the paper, I did research at the Brown University library in Providence. On weekends, my parents would pick me up along with my partner, Sister Mary Thomas, and drive us to Brown. We could not have lunch together or even have something to drink with them. But it was great to have more time together. I remember thinking then that I could study math for the rest of my life. I loved digging into material and following a new idea to new places. It was great.

However, the highlight of my life at Salve Regina was a part-time professor who came from Brown University and taught a course in abstract algebra. I loved it! And, because of him, I still have a passion for the subject. Once again, only the four of us were in the class. Arlene thought he was really cute. I thought he was, too, but didn't say so. He was also a dynamic teacher and so bright. Because there were so few of us, he decided to give an oral final exam. Oh, my God! I was really scared. I remember the four of us sitting outside the room waiting our turns to be tested. I wasn't first or last, I think I was third. But I remember going into the room and found him sitting on a desk, his long legs folded up almost to his chin. Then he had me go to the board and he gave me a theorem to prove on the board. I did okay with the first one and we went on to others. I loved it. Whenever I hesitated, he asked leading questions and I finished the proof. You can imagine how I proud I was of that A. Most auspicious.

Because I majored in math, I didn't have to spend a lot time researching and writing papers. So I went to the periodical room in the library and read everything I could get my hands on. Our periodical room was the ballroom of McAuley Hall. Formerly the home of Florence Vanderbilt Twombly, "Vinland" is next door to the Breakers, where her brother, Cornelius, lived. The ballroom, now our periodical room, had high ceilings festooned with elaborate gold molding and a wall of floor to ceiling windows that overlooked Cliff Walk and just beyond, the Atlantic Ocean. Many of the windows opened to the expansive patios surrounding McAuley Hall. From the patio, lush green lawn flowed down to the Cliff Walk of Newport, all that separated us from the ocean. I loved studying there.

As math majors we were required to take a year of physics and we did this as seniors. Dr. Morris taught the class and we all loved him. He was married to the sister of a nun in our community and they had two children. He was easy on the eyes, very easy, and a great teacher as well. That class met at the end of the day so we couldn't make the bus back to Bay View. Dr. Morris volunteered to drive us on the three days a week that class met. Those drives home were so much fun. We talked about everything from religion, to politics, to physics, to philosophy. He was wonderful. I learned so much in his class and on the rides home.

There is one thing though, about him and his class that stuck in my craw and still does to this day. The final exam in June was pretty straightforward and I remember working on a force problem where I knew the answer should be a negative force but no matter how many times I checked my work I couldn't get it to come out mathematically to be negative. So I just put the negative sign in front of my solution. When I got back the exam, my grade was 95%. He had taken off 5 points on the force problem for as he put it "using my intuition." I am still mad about that.

As part of a religious studies class at Salve, we read The Nun in the World by Cardinal Leon Joseph Suenens and spent time critiquing it. I was totally fascinated by his premise, that religious life had lost the direction of its founders, and had become more secular. At the same time, there was upheaval in the priesthood also. Andrew Greeley, a parish priest in Chicago, wrote articles for "America," a journal published by the Jesuits. Greeley referred to young sisters in Religious Life as a "New Breed," young people who questioned the tenets of their religious orders. I looked forward to his articles every week. I also read Time, Newsweek, US News and World Report and every other periodical with political news. As a result, I began to question my role as a Sister of St. Edmund. If Mother Jordan were here now, what would she think of what we were doing? In spite of the fact that I began to question my religious life, I didn't do anything to really change it. I lived it as I always had.

Early morning of Friday, November 22, 1963, found us on the bus to Salve Regina College in Newport for our regular classes. The day went well and after lunch, I went to the library as usual to check out the periodicals. When I passed the circulation desk, one of the nuns said she had just heard on the radio that President Kennedy had been shot. How can that be? Impossible. We gathered around the radio and listened to the worsening reports, silent, devastated. I stood there till a little after two and then left to walk back across campus to get the bus back to the juniorate. Every day, the sea breezes gently moved the flag in front of the main building, Ochre Court. As I walked, the flag was lowered to half-mast, slowly, all the way down, all the way up, and finally, half way back down. That image is in my mind today as clear as the day it happened almost fifty years ago.

We rode home in stunned silence, some of us quietly crying, full of dread for our country and concern for his young family. Once we arrived at St. Anslem's, we went to the kitchen where Al had a TV on and watched the news as we prepared dinner. Total confusion, chaos, hardened newsmen filling up with tears as they spoke. Constant coverage provided glimpses of Jackie. I still remember Bobby meeting her at the airport and helping her down from Air Force One in back of the President's coffin. She walked to the hearse and tried to open the door but couldn't seem to find the handle. She was still covered in his blood. So young, so valiant. We were fortunate to have her carry us through the days to follow.

The TV was on in the recreation room of the juniorate for the next three days. Every time we weren't in chapel or preparing meals, we were there in front of it. Such a short time ago we had been all together in front of another TV watching his unforgettable Inaugural Address.

The flag at Salve remained at half-mast for a month - as flags did across the country. The world became a sadder place with the loss of our young and gallant leader. It was so hard to pick up again and return to classes. But we did.

One of my math classes that final semester was modern geometry and I loved it. For the first time, I learned that there were other geometries besides Euclidean and was totally fascinated. You can imagine how excited I was years later to study fractal geometry. I wish everyone loved math the way I do. Ah, well.

On June 3, 1964, my parents celebrated their twenty-fifth wedding anniversary. They planned an Anniversary Mass at St. Augustine's Church in Providence, followed by a dinner for family and friends at a nearby restaurant. They asked Sister Mary Stella if I could participate in the celebration and were thrilled that I would be able to attend the Mass. My partner was Sister Mary Nora, Alice Shanahan from Zone Street. Her parents also attended the celebration. It was made clear to my parents that I would not be allowed to attend the dinner nor was I allowed to visit my parents' home just around the corner from the Church. Once we had left home, we were never allowed to return. It was just short of a miracle that I was allowed to attend the Mass with Mom and Dad. The day could not have been more beautiful. It was just perfect. My parents picked up Sister Mary Nora and me and drove us to the Church. It was filled with family and friends of my parents, there to share with them in this happy day. Little did I know then that I would walk down that same aisle six years later as a real bride to meet my husband.

After Mass, Sister Mary Nora and I were driven back to St. Anselm's while everyone else joined my parents in the celebratory dinner.

At the end of the summer of 1964, a separate graduation for the nuns was held at Salve Regina at Ochre Court. We were not allowed to graduate with the girls. My parents came, along with my aunts and uncles and even my great aunt and great uncle. I was the first person in my family to graduate from college. My Dad was especially proud. I remember that. It was a beautiful day, and we marched from the Great Hall outside under the carriage arch and beside Ochre Court to the patio overlooking Cliff Walk and the ocean. I remember being there, and a feeling of pride and happiness for my parents, but I don't remember much else. My great aunt and uncle gave me a pair of Abraham Lincoln bookends for graduation and I still have them. We had a speaker; I don't remember whom, and we each walked up to get our degrees. Sister Mary Philip graduated magna cum laude. I think Sister Mary Simon graduated cum laude. I graduated softly.

After graduation, we all went our separate ways according to the assignments given to us by Mother Provincial. Sister Mary Philip and I went to Massachusetts. I went to Fall River and she went to New Bedford. She was going to teach history to high school kids, just about four or five years younger than she. I was going to teach grades seven and eight.

Sister Mary Philip's mother drove us to our first missions; that's what we called our assignments after graduating from college. It was a long ride. We were both scared. They dropped me off at the door of St. Thomas's Convent in Fall River, after making sure someone was there to let me in. The first person I met was Sister Mary Dominic, the person who would be my first principal.

CHAPTER FIVE

Initiation

St. Thomas's Convent was in the north end of Fall River, Massachusetts, at the foot of a hill. It was an odd-shaped house with two floors, a basement, and a chapel. The front door opened into a tiny hallway, which led into the front parlor. The parlor was on your left as you entered the house and had windows on two sides. Off the parlor to the right was the piano room, so called because the piano was there and that's where Sister Mary Mercedes gave lessons. From the parlor a long hall extended to the chapel at the back of the house. The first door on the left next to the parlor was the superior's office. Opposite the superior's office was the kitchen, Sister Mary Jude's kingdom, as I was soon to discover. She was short but she was powerful. Most convents did not have a cook, but we did and I came to love her. The map of Ireland covered her face and her brogue was still very thick even after almost a lifetime in America. Sister Mary Jude was old and a little stooped over. She had to look up when she spoke to almost everyone.

Beyond the kitchen, still on the right side of the house was the refectory, sort of a double room, connected to the kitchen by a sizeable pantry. A rather comfortable room was added onto the left side of the house where we had a television and enough comfortable chairs for all of us to gather for activities as opposite as chapter and recreation. The chapel and sacristy completed the first floor. Upstairs the long hall separated the cells along each side of the house. My cell was on the side facing the school. As a matter of fact, I could look into my classroom from my bed. My cell was quite lavish because it had a sink. How great was that! Of course, there was also the bed and a chest of drawers, actual walls, (no more curtains) and a door. There was only one full bathroom but that wasn't too bad since there were so few of us. And I think the old nuns didn't take that many showers.

All of the nuns at St. Thomas's were sixty-three years old or above, except Sister Mary Martha, twenty-four, and Sister Mary William, twenty-six. I was twenty-three. Sister Mary William was a little odd, an artist. Sister Mary Dominic was the principal, and then we had Sister Mary Edward, Sister Mary Mercedes, Sister Mary Peter, the superior, Sister Mary Thaddeus, Sister Mary Jude, born in Ireland, and Sister Mary Brendan, also from Ireland, who became a friend until she died several years later. She attended my wedding.

My own classroom! At long last I would begin teaching math, science, music, and religion to seventh and eighth graders. I had never been in a classroom before, not as a teacher anyway. And I was terrified.

Thank God I had a fabulous class my first year of teaching. I still remember so many of them: Bonnie Sanderson, Timothy Feeny, Jane Ryan, David Sheathelm, Bronwyn Hardisty, Max Trask. I taught math and science and Sister Mary Thaddeus taught history and English. She scared the bejesus out of me so I can't even imagine the effect she had on the kids. She definitely did not like me or the way I taught. As far as she was concerned, I couldn't do anything right.

I think we had about three weeks before school began and so we started setting up our classrooms and doing lesson plans. Sister Mary Martha was a great help. I had never been in a classroom before and I was assigned to teach math and science to seventh and eighth grade, music (if you can imagine), art and, of course, religion. My first year was surprisingly easy. The students were fabulous and the parents loved everything I did. Probably because I was young and the nuns their children had in the past were all over sixty. Sister Mary Thaddeus had the eighth grade homeroom and I had the seventh. Music was an absolute challenge for me since I am tone deaf, can't sing, and know nothing about anything except Elvis, the Beach Boys, Pat

Boone, and the Platters. Soooo, I decided to "teach" classical music. I borrowed some LP's from the convent and played The Brandenburg Concerto along with a few other classical pieces. I was pathetic. Ever since, every music teacher I have ever known I regard with the utmost respect - well, almost every one. Talk about math anxiety – I had music anxiety. Art wasn't so bad because I had Sister Mary William, who was an artist. She gave me great ideas and I just followed what she said to do. So teaching was good for me in so many ways.

Sister Mary Martha and I had to take classes at Sacred Heart on Saturday mornings in order to teach the new science and math programs. The math was cake for me but the science was more difficult. Anyway, we had a great time going together on Saturday mornings. We'd walk to Sacred Heart where the classes were held. This involved climbing a huge hill to get there and then walking along its crest where we had a great view of the city. I loved those walks, especially in the fall.

I remember Father Kelly, one of the parish priests, offering to give us a ride there in his Volkswagen Carmengia. But Sister Mary Martha and I refused. She was six four and I am five six so there is no way we could fit. I thought Father Kelly was sweet on Sister Martha. He would join us during recess in the schoolyard and play wall ball with us and the students. It was so much fun! Everyone would be jumping for the ball and we would crash into each other. His eyes, always his eyes, laughing, so much fun.

At St. Thomas's parish there were three priests, a pastor and two curates. That was the usual set up in the fifties and sixties. Our pastor was Father O'Keefe, short and round like Santa Claus without the beard, and the curates were Father Paul Kelly and Father Thomas Johnson. The parish centered around the church physically and emotionally. The church and rectory faced Main Street and the school and convent faced North High Street, but were backed up to the church and rectory. The rectory and convent shared the parking lot, which extended from Weetamoe Street to the convent and from the back of the church to North High Street. So much happened there.

45

I first met Father Kelly soon after I arrived at St. Thomas's. He was introduced to me along with the pastor, Father O'Keefe and the other curate, Father Johnson. I remember his eyes, alive blue, twinkling: the devil in them as well as extraordinary caring and intelligence. The priests took turns saying Mass in the convent. During my first year there I didn't have much to do with Father Kelly because I was so totally involved in learning how to teach. At this time I had no idea how my eventual relationship with him would affect the rest of my life.

What was life like "on the missions?" Actually, it wasn't that bad. There were no responsibilities. I was told what to do and for the most part I did it. I had a roof over my head, food in my belly, clothes to wear, and no decisions to make. I had to teach and pretty much did my own thing there. As long as I covered the material they were okay with what I did.

Every morning we woke up to a knock on our cell door and "Lord Jesus preserve us in peace." to which we responded, "Amen." That's how the nun whose turn it was knew we were awake. The "convent crier" knocked on everyone's door with the same message. At St. Thomas's, since we had sinks in our cells, we could brush our teeth there and then use the bathroom down the hall. We put on our habits after we took off our flannel nightgowns. I was never completely naked. I started to dress by unbuttoning the top of my nightgown, slipping my arms out of the sleeves, and pulling it to my waist. Then I put on my corset over the cotton nightshirt that I also slept in. Once the corset was in place, I stepped out of the nightgown, picked it up and neatly folded it. Yes, it was a flesh colored corset with bones that laced in the front. (I still took out the "bones" for comfort.) We did not wear bras because the corset provided "lift," such as it was. And it didn't matter anyway because the flammable guimp worn around our necks covered our breasts. I am still uncomfortable using "breast" in connection with dressing. Unbelievable. After the corset, we put on the black habit that hooked up the front from just above the waist. Next came the guimp, followed by the coif and veil. The cincture went around our waists and from it hung a long strap (the source of great fear among our students – I've always thought a little fear was healthy) and a huge rosary (which I loved to swing around and around when no one was looking). The black cotton stockings hooked to the garters attached to the corset. Our black lace tied shoes sported chunky heels. No Prada for us! Finally, the big black sleeves buttoned to the top of each shoulder, adding yet more warmth. This is what we wore all year round. Let me tell you, I was hot.

As you can imagine, it took some time to put on the entire habit. I never had a coat in the convent. We did have beautiful cloaks that went under the guimp and over the habit. I loved wearing that because I felt regal in it. However, we didn't wear them very often. Instead, in the winter months we wore a sweater over our habits. I remember my Aunt Agnes made me a beautiful black wool sweater that I wore under the guimp. It kept me warm.

After checking to be sure I had everything on, I went down to chapel for office. The chapel was small and cozy. When I arrived I genuflected and knelt on my prie dieu to say a prayer. We took turns leading the morning office, which was said very differently from the way we did it in the novitiate. In the novitiate we chanted the office and it was quite pious. Here, "on the missions," it was less pious and more "let's get it done." The priest would arrive to say Mass while the youngest nuns went to hang out the laundry during the last part of the office. Ah. The laundry. There were articles of clothing that the old nuns wore which I still can't figure out. Some of them looked like flags with holes in them. I was mortified having to hang them out because, invariably, when I was out there at the clothesline, the priest would come across the parking lot to the convent to say Mass. I remember fervently hoping he didn't think these things were mine!

Mass was also somewhat abbreviated and Sister Mary Jude, our cook, left before it was over to prepare breakfast. After Mass we had breakfast, always delicious. Sister Mary Jude was a great cook. And then off to teach. The school was about twenty feet from the convent. As a matter of fact, when I was sick, I could watch my students in the classroom from my cell window. School was escape into the real world. I totally loved teaching.

After school, I usually stayed in my classroom until I finished preparing for the next day and then went back to the convent to start the afternoon charges. Because we had such a senior group of nuns, Sister Mary Martha, Sister Mary William – we called her Willy - and I had to do everything. One of the charges of the young nuns was the aforementioned laundry. Now, there were pieces of underwear that came through our washing the likes of which I had never seen. Huge billowing pantaloons that had to be ironed, mind you, and ironed just so or we had to do them over. Fortunately, we did not have to cook, because we had Sister Mary Jude. She took a liking to Sister Martha and me, often asking us to "sample" her cookies, but she never really warmed up to Willy. We had such a great time with her. And what a cook she was. No Sunday buns, though. They were a thing of the past.

Every Sunday night, I had to give my lesson plans to Sister Mary Dominic, the principal, for her to check. They were always fine. I still can't believe that I never put a foot in the classroom till my first day on my own. Although I was scared, I loved it from the first day.

The students sat in six rows across with eight seats in each row. To start out, I had them sit in alphabetical order so I could learn their names. Before school started, I put their names in my grade book. That grade book made me feel like a "real teacher." Armed with it, my plan book, and some textbooks, I headed over to school to meet my first class. I wonder if they knew how totally inexperienced I was. They probably did, but didn't show it. Thinking about them now, I wonder what happened to them. They are in their mid-fifties. I wonder if they ever think of that year we had together. I do! I remember so many of them.

One of my students that year, Eric Swanson, got into some serious trouble. He was found on the street, half dead from drinking a fifth of whiskey. Can you imagine? Where on God's green earth would he even get it? Well, he wound up having to appear in court before a judge. His lawyer asked me if I would be a character witness for him and of course I said yes. Sister Mary Martha came to court with me (we always had to travel with a partner) but she waited outside the judge's chambers. I don't know how scared Eric was of the judge, but I was definitely subdued. He was huge – the judge – and the voluminous, flowing robes did nothing to minimize his figure. I just answered the judge's questions yea or nay. Eric was a really quiet, well-behaved boy in my class. I hardly knew he was there. But I liked him a lot. There was something endearing about him. I wonder what ever happened to him. I hope he's okay.

Teaching seemed to come naturally to me. Classes were fun and the students were learning. One of the difficulties for me that year was designing tests that accurately measured what they were learning. I made my tests too hard at first and students who had always done well were getting C's and D's. Not so good. I was especially bad at making up science tests. I remember one student, Susan Hardisty, getting a C on a science test and her aunt, also a Sister of St. Edmund, looked at the test and told me it was too hard. But I got better as the year went on.

I loved teaching math. And it was the very best time to be teaching it and because of the "space race," emphasis was placed on math and science. It was the "New Math" and I loved every bit of it. Different bases, symbolic logic, modular arithmetic, geometry, figuring out the WHY, not just HOW, to do it. Parents had some difficulty figuring it out and if I had had more experience at that point, I would have held a parent meeting to explain to them what the new math was.

The Saturday morning classes really helped me with teaching science. I loved teaching chemistry because it was so mathematical, but anything beyond that was a struggle for me. So I did a unit on the space program and had the students memorize the names of the original seven astronauts. I had bulletin boards covered with photos from space and the kids loved it.

Preparing for my first parent conferences made me a little anxious. I wanted to let the parents know I was competent. Not so easy given my total lack of experience. But they all showed up and were pretty nice to me. Thank God.

Classes were going well and I planned a field trip to New York City in May for the class. I knew the children would not have money readily available, so I started planning early to give them a chance to earn the money. We would take the train from Providence, Rhode Island, to Grand Central Station and walk to the United Nations Building for a guided tour. Afterward we would have lunch at the automat. My mother agreed to chaperone with me and the date was set. Actually it was my birthday, May 29, 1965. It was the first time some of the children had ever been out of Fall River. I remember one mom thanking me for letting the families know so early because she wanted to save the money and give it to her daughter because her daughter had been so helpful: babysitting, house cleaning, and doing anything to help her mom, whose husband had recently passed away. I wonder what ever became of Jenny.

The day finally arrived and we were off to the big city. My Mom and I had the best time. The kids were great and they even sang Happy Birthday to me on the train. We had about 30 kids and got off the train and walked through Grand Central Station. There were so many tourists, totally enjoying the beautiful building and all the sights. We turned left and headed down to the UN Wow! The sidewalks were so wide. Look at the huge buildings! The students were so great on the tour of the UN. After the tour, we visited the gift shop. Every single child bought a souvenir for their mom. We started out back toward Grand Central Station. As we walked into Grand Central, Leo Baldwin walked out and I nearly fainted. He had gotten lost when we left Grand Central in the morning and was there, alone, the whole day. I almost died. My mother blanched and then hugged him and asked him if he was okay. When I think of what could have happened. He could have been sold into white slavery never to be seen again. I will never forget that experience as long as I live.

Another advantage of life on the missions was visiting day. My parents and family members came once a month to see me in the front parlor of the convent. Sister Mary Jude even made a snack for them; however, I was still not allowed to eat in front of the laity.

My friend, Sister Mary Philip, was stationed in New Bedford and when we could get a ride, we tried to visit each other. She was teaching history to high school students and we shared with each other our experiences in the classroom and in convent life. It was a shock to both of us how lax life on the missions was. But we were adjusting and making out okay. It was so good to see her and just talk together.

Sometime during that first year at St. Thomas's, I began to feel an ache in me, a longing for intimacy that I had never felt before. It came and went from time to time, surprising me at times with its intensity. I was twenty-four years old and a nun. Was I sinning by having these thoughts?

That summer when school was out, I was assigned to St. Mark's Home in Fall River, Massachusetts. I wonder if it's still there. It was a home for children who had been in trouble or who had no families, sort of an orphanage. That was an eye-opening experience for me. I was there the whole summer but I can't remember much of what I did there. The children were divided by sex and age into groups and placed in dorms throughout the orphanage. The dorms had beds lined up against both walls and a large space down the center. Each child had a chest of drawers where they kept their things.

I remember one especially harsh nun who was in charge of the little boys, aged three to six. I can still see her standing at the doorway of the dorm lining up the boys and cracking them on their legs with a thick, wooden ruler if they were slow to get in line. And I didn't do anything about it. She was awful. I was responsible for the teenage girls; there were only a few of them, maybe four or five. I vaguely remember going out onto the railroad tracks, which ran in back of the home, to find a missing teenage girl.

I also remember Father Kelly coming to say daily Mass. It felt good to see him. We didn't speak, but waved to each other in passing. It was good to see someone from "home." I thought several of the nuns there were really mean to the children, imposing really harsh punishments. It was not a pleasant experience.

After finishing up at St. Mark's, I joined my band back at the novitiate in Cumberland, Rhode Island, to renew my vows for two more years. We shared stories of our experiences on the missions and how we coped with the very different life there compared to the novitiate or juniorate. The renewal ceremony was on August 16, just three years since our first vows. Many changes had taken place in our lives. Life on the missions was very different from our life in the novitiate. Life in the novitiate was cloistered, regimented, focused on growth in love of God. On the missions we found that religious life was more lax than we thought it would be. I wonder if we were at the brink of disillusionment about religious life?

The renewal ceremony for us was not huge. Rather, the big events on August 15 and 16 were reception, first vows, and final vows. We had a retreat before and time to consider the step we were about to take. I did not even think about anything but renewing my vows. I still was in for the duration.

After renewing our vows, we went to The Villa again in Dartmouth, Massachusetts, for a week long vacation. It was good to be back there for our vacation. Let me tell you, it was something to see the bathing attire of the nuns. This year it wasn't just the nuns from the novitiate; it was nuns from the entire order. Again, we had to wear bathing caps to cover our baldness. The swimming "dresses" were a hoot. Some of the older nuns had no skin showing at all. I thought they would drown with the weight of their outfits. The nuns in my band again wore our gym suits from high school; that is, if our parents hadn't already thrown them out. We all got sunburned beyond belief and suffered immeasurably with it. As luck would have it, I got my period during the ONE week of the year that I could go swimming. Fortunately, our band shared a room on the third floor of The Villa and Sister Mary James Patrick showed me how to use a tampon. Where she learned, I never asked. Holy smoke. I thought I was breaking my vow of chastity. It took me about seven tries before I got it in. At least I could go swimming.

There aren't that many decisions in one's life that are really huge. For me, one of them was to enter the convent. The decision to go to St. Thomas's, Fall River, however, was not mine. What would my life have been like had I been sent to any other place? How could the superiors know what effect their decision would eventually have on my life and on so many others? One switch between me and any other member of my band. I wonder if they subsequently thought about that.

CHAPTER SIX

Reality Sets In

As my second year at St. Thomas's began, I found a new community waiting. Sister Mary Jude, our cook, left and Sister Mary Albert, Sister Marie Luke, Sister Mary Matthew and Sister Mary Rose arrived. Sister Mary Matthew and Sister Mary Rose were respectively the superintendent and assistant superintendent of schools for the diocese of Fall River and had requested from the Mother Provincial that they be assigned to our convent because we had such a good reputation. They had weird schedules because of their responsibilities and were in and out all the time. Sister Mary Albert was a year behind me in the novitiate, so she was a year younger than I. Sister Mary Peter became principal and remained superior. She was an extraordinary principal. I learned so much from her about what it means to be a teacher.

The school year began with little fanfare but I soon realized that this class was far different from last year's class. They were unbelievably wild and I had no idea how to handle them. Last year's class had spoiled me. It eventually became so bad for me that I dreaded going to school every day and could barely get through a lesson without some disaster or other happening. I wanted to quit teaching so badly but, of course, I couldn't. Obedience is big in the convent. I was almost totally incapable of teaching. Every morning I woke up dreading the upcoming day. Hours and hours of planning were to no avail. No matter what I tried, it just always came up short.

One of my most difficult students was Kevin Mercer. He threw a desk across the classroom. He picked it up and literally threw it across the room. It was unbelievable. I know it was an especially difficult time for him because his dad was dying of cancer and he just didn't know how to handle it. What twelve-year-old boy would? Father Kelly was trying to work with him and his family, without much success. His dad finally died but the situation was not much better after that. Mr. Mercer's wake was huge and I made such a faux pas because I said to his older brother, "Now it would be easier." How stupid was that? Talk about sympathetic.

Sister Mary Peter was a huge support for me during that year. It was so bad for me that I just wanted to quit and become the convent cook. But she stuck with me and I hobbled through the year, every morning dreading the upcoming day. I had absolutely no control of the class and they knew it. I barely survived. Sister Mary Peter and I would spend time together and she would share with me her philosophy of teaching. Her first precept was to remember that each child was loved by his or her parents, was very unique, and deserved our respect. She also believed that planning and preparation were the best antidotes to discipline problems. In other words, if I spent enough time planning really good lessons, the students would be engaged and not as likely to create problems. She also believed in not smiling until Thanksgiving, but I could never make it that long. And it was already too late for that year.

During this year at St. Thomas's, the newly arrived Sister Marie Luke played an important role. Sister Marie Luke was thirty-two, so considered one of the young nuns in the group. She was very tall, about six feet, with a dark complexion, a pointed nose and always seemed a little scary to me. And she was an alcoholic and a little bit crazy. Her cell was next to mine and I saw her take the altar wine from the sacristy into her cell in the evening. That was a shock. Religious life on the missions was definitely not what I had experienced in the novitiate. Because I am not too bright when it comes to observing people, I did not realize that Sister Marie Luke was also a lesbian. Actually, I didn't even know such a thing existed. She sought out Sister Mary Peter, our superior and principal. I developed a really great relationship with Sister Mary Peter and found myself jealous of Sister Marie Luke. She was always in Sister Mary Peter's office, talking with her about this and that. Eventually, Father Kelly got involved with the situation and suggested to Sister Mary Peter that Sister Marie Luke see a psychiatrist and so she and Sister Mary Peter went to see the doctor at least once a week. The doctor was located in New Hampshire and I envied the time they had together traveling back and forth. So, in order to get some of Sister Mary Peter's attention, I developed a "lump" at the base of my breastbone and went with Peter to see Dr. McCook in Fall River. Dr. McCook was a friend of Father Kelly's and the doctor's children all went to St. Thomas's School. He checked me out and said that it really wasn't anything but if I wanted to have it removed, he could do it. I decided not to. After all, I had achieved what I wanted, Sister Mary Peter's attention, if only for a little while. I loved her and so wanted to please her.

Sister Mary Martha and I liked to visit the shut-ins in St. Thomas's Parish. We would ask the priests for a list of people who might like a visit and then walk to their homes after school was out. Those times together with her meant so much to me. I think we walked on every single street in St. Thomas's parish and, in the process, became a familiar sight to the people there. What a pair we made. She was so tall and we both were quite energetic, never slowing our pace till we arrived at the person's home. The people were so appreciative of our taking the time to see them. Some were grandparents of our students, but most were homebound and hungry for human interaction. It was a great time for us. We were fulfilling the mission of Mother Jordan by performing one of the corporal works of mercy, visiting the sick. We had become nuns in the world.

At one point during that year, Father Kelly had to go to St. Anne's Hospital to have a hemorrhoid removed. Sister Mary Martha and I went to visit him after the procedure. What a sight he was, lying on his belly and clearly embarrassed to have us see him like that. But we made light of it and had a fun visit.

Sister Marie Luke was another story. One night, she came flying out of Sister Mary Peter's cell, all a dither, habit askew, face contorted, and Sister Mary Peter with blood coming out her mouth. I have no idea what happened but it wasn't good. Soon after that, Father Kelly met with Sister Mary Albert and me in Sister Mary Peter's office. He asked me if Sister Marie Luke had ever tried to touch us and while I hadn't thought of it before, she had put hand under my guimp on my breasts and up to my neck, apparently trying to warm up her hands. How naive was I.

The miserable teaching situation combined with the Sister Marie Luke situation was awful. My life was the pits. Prayer did not help much either. I barely survived.

Sister Mary Albert was very pious, just out of the juniorate. Anyway, we were the youngest, and had all the s___ jobs. One day in the fall of that year, Monsignor O'Keefe called and said that a monsignor had died on Long Island and his family (who were from our parish) wanted his wake and funeral here at St. Thomas's Church. In those days it meant that someone had to sit with the body around the clock until the solemn funeral Mass. Of course, there weren't enough priests to do it so the nuns had to take turns. Sister Mary Albert and I had from two to three in the morning. Now, Fall River, Massachusetts, in those days was no Shangri-La. I was a little wary of going over there in the middle of the night. After all, I had my virtue to protect. So I met Sister Mary Albert in the downstairs hallway and told her I was going to the kitchen to get a knife to take with me to the wake.

Well, she was scandalized for two reasons: one, talking during the Grand Silence – me, not her - and two, the idea of taking a knife was beyond her. I didn't care. Remember my virtue? So off we went to "watch" the monsignor with the carving knife secure in my very large pocket. The pocket tied around our waist over the corset and under the habit. It was sort of like a giant pouch and could hold all sorts of things. Like a carving knife.

St. Thomas's Church is a rather imposing church, sort of a small cathedral. So you can imagine my shock when we opened the doors and went into the church to see his royal highness laid out fully extended and up on a slant so that I almost looked into his eyes. They were closed. If you've ever seen a pope laid out you'll know what I mean. We walked down the aisle and relieved Sister Mary Brendan and Sister Marie Luke. There was no one else in the entire church. Sister Mary Albert and I started praying, not together, because it was the Grand Silence. It didn't take long for me to get bored. I can only say so many rosaries. I started looking around, especially at HIM. He was regaled in all his finery, brilliant red robes and an alb trimmed with gorgeous lace. He was pretty old. After a while I said to Sister Mary Albert, "I'm going to see what he has on underneath all these robes." Oh, my God! I thought she would have cardiac arrest. I didn't care: who would know? So I got up, looked around the Church to be sure no one else was there, walked over to him, lifted up the lacy alb and almost fainted. He didn't have anything on underneath! Shoes and socks, yes. But nothing else. Can you imagine those priests not putting underwear on him? I said, "Sister Mary Albert, he hasn't got anything on!" She just pretended not to hear me and kept on praying. I can still see that poor, wrinkled man.

One of our parishioners was an elderly gentleman, Henry Wallace. During the fall of that year, he took Sister Mary William and me to Boston for the day in his Lincoln Continental. We had the best time. He suggested that we go the Ritz for tea in the afternoon, but when Sister Mary William and I saw it, we decided we weren't "dressed" for the occasion. So we went to a small restaurant near the Boston Common. Later on, when the nuns could get their licenses and could drive, he gave us the Continental and I drove it everywhere. How edifying was that? Nuns cruising around in a Lincoln Continental. We should have had a sign that said, "donated by Henry Wallace." I think I was the only one who had a license. Fortunately, my mother hadn't let mine lapse. I wonder what she had in mind for me?

Monsignor O'Keefe named Father Kelly Director of the School that year and they decided to create a new school library in the basement of the rectory. This entailed finishing the basement, which they did in no time. I was to be the librarian. I was a math teacher. What was I doing as a librarian? I found out soon enough. The process involved meeting privately with Father Kelly to select shelving, books, and carpeting, which meant spending time together. One afternoon after school Father Kelly came to the convent with carpet samples. He told me to pick out any one I liked for the library floor so I picked out a vibrant blue that seemed to have stars sparkling in it. On another afternoon we picked out the basic set of library books together and when they were delivered I began processing them and putting them on the brand new shelves. Once everything was completed, we had a grand opening for the staff and students. The library turned out to be a wonderful place for the children. They loved leaving school, crossing the parking lot, and going down the steps into their library. I spent my spare time in the library processing books, shelving, etc. One night – I was always alone there – Monsignor O'Keefe came down to see how everything was going. We chatted for a few minutes, wandered through the shelves and then, before he left, he took me in his arms, kissed me quite soundly and said, "I've been waiting a long time to do that." I was stunned! On the lips: he kissed me on the lips. And he's shorter than I am. I never kissed anyone shorter than I am, much less a priest: not just a priest, a MONSIGNOR. Holy smoke. There was never anything between us before that nor was there anything between us afterward. It's so strange. Even now, looking back on it. Priests lead a very lonely life. No wonder vocations have tapered off. That, together with the current sex scandals, may spell the end of the Catholic Priesthood as we know it.

One evening that year the Vienna Boys Choir performed in Fall River at the local theater. Father Kelly gave tickets for the performance to Sister Mary Peter, which she could give to the nuns. So of course the only two that wanted to go were Sister Mary Martha and I. I'm not sure why no else wanted to go, but, that evening, we were thrilled to be on our way. What an occasion! We walked into town and headed into the lobby of the local theater. As we crossed the lobby, I recognized Father Kelly and Father Schmidt, his drop-dead-gorgeous buddy, watching us from across the lobby. I looked at Father Kelly and waved but he didn't wave back. He quickly turned and leapt up the stairs to the mezzanine with Smitty following behind. Sister Mary Martha and I had seats in the orchestra and loved the performance. At intermission, we stayed in our seats but I turned and looked up to see if I could find Father Kelly. I couldn't find him.

My friend, Sister Mary Philip, was transferred from Holy Family High School in New Bedford to St. Patrick's Academy in Providence, Rhode Island. She was thrilled about the change because she had graduated from St. Patrick's and really looked forward to teaching there. I had a new place to visit. The convent at St. Patrick's was huge, dark, and, I thought, rather eerie. Sister Mary Philip and I spent time talking in the gloomy kitchen where I fully expected ghosts of nuns past to appear beside us and chide us for breaking the Grand Silence. We always spoke in subdued whispers so as not to disturb their spirits unnecessarily.

The unsettling winds of Vatican II swept through the Church and into the Sisters of St. Edmund community. Much talk was given to changing the habit because some clergy and religious sisters felt that the habit was off-putting to people. Designs were created and distributed to the nuns for their input. At long last, a decision was made and the new habits were ordered. I really liked them because they were a dark blue and matched my eyes. Vain to the end. Changing from the old habit to the new one entailed an update of underwear. In Fall River, there was only one department store, McWhirr's, and so Sister Mary Martha and I walked into town one afternoon after school to buy bras. I had not worn one since high school and the prospect of buying some new ones was rather exciting. McWhirr's had an escalator and we rode up to the second floor where the bras were organized in small plastic boxes in neat rows and columns by size. We approached the saleslady and I asked to see a plain white bra size 34 B. She turned and quickly found several for me to choose from. Then Sister Mary Martha, six feet two and flat as a pancake, whispered to her that she would like to see a plain white bra also, but size 42 AA. So she turned around and started going up and down the rows of plastic boxes, up and down, but couldn't find any. So she turned and hollered across the floor "GLADYS, HAVE YOU GOT ANY 42 AA's?" I thought Martha would die. She turned purple and I was almost wetting my pants I was laughing so hard.

After the bra episode, came the shoe episode. We would
never have to wear the god-awful, black lace up, clodhoppers
again. So Sister Mary Peter let Sister Mary Martha and me go
back into town to pick out shoes for our new habits. Sister Mary
Peter was afraid that we would come back with black patent
leather stilettos, but we didn't and she was actually quite pleased
with our selection of sensible black shoes with a small club heel.
Now we were ready for the fashion change.

On Sunday morning, we donned our new habits and crossed
the parking lot to attend the children's Mass, regaled in our gorgeous finery. I loved it. I felt feminine. Even though our breasts
were still covered with a bib, it flattered our shape just a little.
Even Father Kelly mentioned our new look in his sermon.

The old nuns were given the option of not changing and
most of the old nuns at St. Thomas's didn't change. Can you
imagine shopping for bras with them???

As the school year wound down - not soon enough for me
- plans were made for the upcoming summer. I was assigned
to stay at St. Thomas's and work in a local program for inner
city kids. The director was a middle-aged Lebanese man and
rather harsh, I thought. He was the principal at the school where
the program was held. The school year finally ended and I had
about a week before the summer program began. I cleaned out
my classroom and my memory of the year. It is rather telling,
too, for me to realize that I can't remember a single student's
name from that year, except Kevin Mercer.

The inner city program in Fall River was for six weeks and
was held in a public school on the south side of the city. Mr.
Garbezian picked me up every morning on Main Street across
from St. Thomas's Church. One morning I was running a little
late and he was really angry. The school was in an Eastern
Orthodox parish and the local priest was also involved in the
summer program. It was nice because he knew all the kids and
they obviously loved him. Well, it seems that Eastern Orthodox
priests can marry. So, one day, a parishioner of the parish invited
Mr. Garbezian, Father Topalian and me to her home for dinner.
We all went and joined a nice group of people for a delicious

meal. During the course of conversation, it was pointed out to me that priests were allowed to marry. Could this possibly be a set up? Unbelievable. My role in the summer program was sort of like a camp counselor, definitely not one of my talents. I survived the six weeks, but was not looking forward to going back to school at St Thomas's.

Before school started, we had a week at The Villa again. Father Kelly offered to take Sister Mary Brendan, Sister Mary William, and me to Martha's Vineyard for a day. He picked us up at the Villa early one morning. My band had been there for the week on vacation. We loved that huge old house on the water and we all enjoyed swimming at the beach there. It was a perfect summer day for the trip. He had borrowed a larger car so we could all fit in it. I sat in the back with Sister Mary Brendan, and Sister Mary William was in the front with Father Kelly. His sister-in-law's family had a home near Woods Hole on Cape Cod and we changed there into our beach clothes. It was a lovely home. We used a bedroom upstairs. I know sister Mary William and I changed but I don't think Sister Mary Brendan did. How funny that I remember that bedroom. We boarded the ferry for the island in Woods Hole and had a wonderful cruise to Vineyard Haven. Father Kelly and I stood together by railing and he pointed out to me the various landmarks: East Chop, Vineyard Haven, and Oak Bluffs. What were these feeling I had for him as we stood together? We took the car on the ferry and, once on the island, we drove to Gay Head, a beach on the far side of the island. Father Kelly had brought everything we needed for a clambake. We set up on the beach and he began to dig a hole for the coals. "Have you ever had a clambake?" he asked me. "No, what is it?" "First, you dig a hole and then you put in the coals, light them and put seaweed over them. Then you pile on the clams, lobster, potatoes, and corn, cover it all up with sand and let it bake in the sand while you sun and swim."

All of a sudden, Sister Mary William got sick, really sick and Father Kelly took her to a nearby convent where she spent the rest of the day. So on the beach it was Father Kelly, Sister Mary Brendan, and I. Gay Head is this vast expanse of glistening sand, waves rolling up on the beach, and endless blue-green ocean. The blue-green water beckoned us and we splashed in the waves forever, laughing, talking, and often innocently touching each other. It felt so good to be with him. He was so handsome and really seemed to want to be with me. The beach was nearly deserted even on this gorgeous day. In back of us were the tall, graceful, sand dunes and hidden beyond the dunes was the Gay Head Motel. Years later, I imagined Paul and me spending endless hours together there and on the beach. That day I had still not acknowledged my feelings for him. Eventually, I would. So it was a nice day, spent together, getting to know a little more about each other with Sister Mary Brendan looking on. Although she and I never spoke of my feelings for Paul, she knew how I felt before I did. I loved her.

Soon we had our clambake and it was fabulous. He had thought of everything. Afterward, we stretched out on the blanket and relaxed next to each other. We probably slept a little. It was wonderful. Father Kelly took photos of us and he later told me had one of me in my bathing suit on his desk in his room in the rectory. He told me I was beautiful. He made me feel loved. Eventually, we left the beach and picked up Sister Mary William. She was quite pale. It was dark by the time we boarded the ferry and we settled in for trip back to the mainland. On board, Father asked me if I would like to meet the captain. I said yes, I would and I went with Paul up to the wheelhouse. The captain let me hold the wheel and Paul was so happy. His eyes asked me to respond, but I didn't, and he quickly turned away and went back down to the main deck.

The rest of the return trip to Woods Hole was quiet. After we changed back to our habits at the house, Father Kelly took us to dinner at the country club where his brother had a membership. It was beautiful. We had a table overlooking the water and, although it was dark, the moon was out and reflected on the water. I ordered prime rib and so did he. I don't remember what the others had. Our trip back to the Villa was uneventful, Sister Mary Brendan trying to keep up the conversation. Paul dropped us off at the door and left.

These so many years later, I wish I had let myself be in love with him that night.

The summer was officially over and I was back to teaching at St. Thomas's. What would happen with Paul and me?

CHAPTER SEVEN

Chastity?

The beginning of my third year at St. Thomas's proved to be happily uneventful. You cannot imagine how terrified I was of returning to the classroom after last year's horrific experience. This year Sister Mary Peter spent a lot of time with me before school started, helping me with suggestions. First of all, she once again suggested I start out by not smiling until Thanksgiving and, while I didn't smile for a long time, it was before Thanksgiving. Secondly, she said that planning lessons well made for a positive learning environment because I would know what to do and how to do it. Also, plan more learning activities than I thought I would need, because "idle hands are the devil's workshop." Finally, she said I should not allow a single misbehavior to go unnoticed. When a student made the slightest move that I didn't want him or her to do, I was all over him. There was no doubt this year who was in charge. And what a difference it made. I could teach and the students could learn. My passion for teaching returned.

Once again the community changed. A new junior, Sister Mary Damien came, as well as Sister Mary Harold, who was from my band. Sister Mary Edwardine returned from the missions in Belize to our St. Thomas's and we hit it off right away. She was a riot - into playing practical jokes. One day she told Father Kelly that a message for him had mistakenly come to the convent. He was to call the number left by the person and pick up a box left for him. So he called the number and was connected with a casket company. Another time, during the Grand Silence, she hid in the shower and when I came in, she jumped out and scared the bejesus out of me. I still owe her for that one.

My partner in crime, Sister Mary Martha, left and so did Sister Mary Edward. Sister Mary Edward was a thousand years old and last year had totally screwed up the report cards for her third grade students. Father Kelly and Sister Mary Peter had to do a lot of damage control with the parents over that. Sister Mary Brendan was still there and she was just great. She was a huge presence and exuded happiness.

Father Kelly said Mass in our convent almost every morning and, since it such a small chapel, and I was the youngest, I had a front prie dieu (kneeler). I could smell his after-shave. When he gave me Holy Communion, I felt his fingers touch my lips and my stomach would do a belly flop. During Mass, just before Communion, he would raise the host and say, "Behold the Lamb of God," and the nuns would respond, "Behold Him who has taken away the sins of the world." Well, one day, he was half asleep and instead said, "Behold the handmaid of the Lord" and we were also half asleep and responded "Be it done unto me according to thy word." We started laughing and literally couldn't stop. It was hysterical. You know how it is when you get laughing in church. There were only eight of us there, and we had to bite our lips when we went up for Communion. That was really hard since we had to open our mouths to receive Communion. Oh God, it was a riot!

Meanwhile, Father Philip Mahoney, a parish priest from Somerset, Massachusetts, a town just across the river, started coming to my classroom during the week to pick up altar boys to serve Mass, usually a funeral or a Month's Mind. In those days, a Month's Mind was a Mass celebrated one month after the deceased's funeral. The Month's Mind Masses were announced in the church bulletin every Sunday and anyone who wanted to attend could. Of course, the deceased's family would be there and a gurney with a cloth over it representing the coffin would be wheeled down the main aisle of the church to the front just before the altar. Father Mahoney and I would talk for a few minutes in the hallway before he gathered the boys for the Mass, and when he brought them back, he often brought me a sandwich or donut or some other little snack. He was drop-dead gorgeous. Think

Paul Newman and Harrison Ford as one gorgeous hunk. Tall, well-built, beautiful eyes, a smile to die for, and hands - masculine hands. One day, Father Kelly came up the stairs and found us talking and laughing together. He joined the conversation and then we all parted to resume our responsibilities. Eventually, one of these men – priests - would have my heart and my virginity.

Sometime in the fall of that year, Father Kelly invited Sister Mary Brendan and me to his parents' home for dinner. His brother Dan, and his family were there. The house was on a hill in Fall River across from a school where there was a large playground. Dan's children were playing there when we arrived. A Clancy Brothers album was playing on the stereo. Paul's parents were warm and welcoming, but I remember being very nervous. Sister Mary Christopher was wonderful and soon had us all laughing around the dining room table with her stories of growing up in Ireland. After dinner, we sat in the living room and talked and listened to music. Paul sat on the floor next to me. I remember the song the Clancy brothers were singing.

FARE THEE WELL MY OWN TRUE LOVE
Farewell to Prince's Landing Stage
River Mersey, fare thee well
I am bound for California
A place I know right well
So fare thee well, my own true love
When I return united we will be
It's not the leaving of Liverpool that's grieving me
But my darling when I think of thee
For I think it will be a long, long time
Before I see you again
Oh the sun is on the harbor, love
And I wish I could remain
For I know it will be a long, long time
Till I see you again

*(Also known as "The Leaving of Liverpool"
Roud 9435, a folk ballad)*

I remember a day that fall when Sister Mary Philip and I were visiting Sister Mary George, and we were sitting on the porch of Saint Patrick's Convent in Providence. The night before we had watched the Miss America Pageant on television and were talking about it. Our conversation turned to our lives in the convent and Sister Mary George asked, "What if we're wrong? What if all this sacrifice is for nothing? Suppose we're wasting our lives?" I had never thought about it, well, maybe I had just a little. I still assumed that what we were doing was the best possible thing we could do with our lives. Although, I must admit, I had begun to think that our lives really were pretty easy. Except for the no sex part. We were fed and clothed, we didn't have any decisions to make, and we just did what we were told. In many cases, we were better off than the people we were supposed to be serving. There seemed to be a disconnect between what we were professing and what we were doing. That day, after tossing around some ideas, Sister Mary George and I decided we would volunteer for the missions. We decided that we would ask Mother Christopher to go to Brownsville, Texas, to the parish where Father Paul Kelly's brother, Father Joseph Kelly, was. We felt that at least there we could make a difference. Sister Mary George was a bright young woman totally committed to religious life. Serving in Brownsville would fulfill our innermost need to serve the poor, make a difference in their lives, and help them become self-sufficient. Our idea was submitted to Mother Provincial who sent Mother Christopher, my Mistress of Novices, to see me at St. Thomas's. Mother Christopher asked me why I wanted to try this new mission and I told her to more closely imitate Mother Jordan, to return to the original purpose of our order. She wanted to know if it had anything to do with my relationship with Father Kelly. I was stunned. There was no relationship. Yet, someone in the convent must have reported to the Provincial House what she saw or thought she saw. I was still in the mindset of fighting the feelings I had for Paul. I was an emotional wreck. After she left, I met my parents, who were taking me out for dinner. My Mom noticed how upset I was and had seen Mother Christopher as she was leaving the convent.

I told her I was okay, but she knew I wasn't. The high muck a mucks considered our request and denied it. I'm sure it was partially because they thought I was involved with Father Kelly. Wouldn't you thing that they would let me go to the missions if for no other reason than to separate me from Father Kelly. But they didn't probably because they felt my motives weren't pure. I wonder what my life would have been like if they had allowed me to go to Brownsville? (Joe Kelly was not as good looking as Paul.)

The first year at St. Thomas's, I thought Father Kelly was interested in Sister Mary Martha. Feelings for him were slowly growing in me, but, trying to be a good nun, I fought them daily. He was so handsome; I could melt into his eyes every time he looked at me, which was often.

Because he was the director of the school, I had the opportunity to interact with him a lot. This year Father Kelly decided to start teaching a class once a week to my eighth grade students. It was a class where he talked about feelings, relationships, and attitudes. I stayed in the classroom while he taught it. It was supposedly for the thirteen year olds in my class. I'm sure they got a lot out of it, but so did I. The particular class was really special and they looked forward to him coming. He was a wonderful role model for the boys. He talked about relationships with parents, friends, and teachers. He really helped them all become more sensitive. I remember a story he told about an older couple who were out walking in the park. They held each other's hands as they walked along. Paul said that although the physical passion was probably not as strong as it once was, what nourished their love were their memories of their time together. It was beautiful.

Sometimes I felt he was speaking directly to me. And I discovered later that he was. He would write to me, notes about this or that and always mentioning how he felt for me. The notes would be on my desk after he finished teaching my students and he signed them "Paul." I shared them with Sister Mary Peter – I really did not want to give in to my feelings for him – and somehow or other he found out that she knew. She may have spoken to him about his feelings for me; I don't know. The next lesson he taught in my classroom was on betrayal. How would you feel, he asked the students, if you had shared something personal with a person you cared very much about and that person showed them with someone else. The students all felt that it was a terrible thing to do. After class, I stepped out of the classroom to apologize to him. I felt awful.

Then I found out that Sister Mary Peter and Sister Marie Luke had been listening over the intercom to every class he taught in my classroom. I couldn't believe it. I felt betrayed by Sister Mary Peter, the one I so admired, so longed to emulate. She didn't believe that I was sincere in turning away from Father Kelly's advances. I was so hurt by her lack of trust in me. His advances were so sweet and simple and loving. But I still did not respond.

Day after day I prayed, taught, did chores, visited the sick, and tried to close myself to the feelings for him that were becoming ever so strong. What finally snapped, what finally allowed me to open my heart to him? Sister Mary Matthew asked me to sit down with her and talk. She told me that what I was doing with Father Kelly was causing much trouble in the convent and that I should stop communicating with him. So I decided that since they thought I was involved with him, I might as well validate their thinking. At last I wrote Paul a note expressing that I felt something for him, something special. I put the note in his drawer in the sacristy and waited for his response. It couldn't have been better.

When he came out to say Mass that Sunday morning, he looked at me with so much love in his eyes that I melted inside. I could barely sit and stand at the appropriate times during the service. His sermon was about a desert flower. The desert is so vast and there are so few flowers that when you find one of exquisite beauty, you don't pluck it, but rather leave it there for everyone to see.

From that day, he called me his Desert Flower. Utter joy filled my whole being. He loved me and I loved him. The words of a song from Camelot rang true for me.

I loved you once in silence
And mis'ry was all I knew.
Trying so to keep my love from showing,
All the while not knowing you loved me too.
Yes, loved me in lonesome silence;
Your heart filled with dark despair.
Thinking love would flame in you forever,
And I'd never, never know the flame was there.
Then one day we cast away our secret longing;
The raging tide we held inside would hold no more.
The silence at last was broken!
We flung wide our prison door.
Ev'ry joyous word of love was spoken.
And now there's twice as much grief,
Twice the strain for us;
Twice the despair,
Twice the pain for us
As we had known before.
And after all had been said,
Here we are, my love,
Silent once more,
And not far, my love,
From where we were before.

(From "Camelot", book and lyrics by Alan Jay Lerner and music by Frederick Loewe)

For the first time in my life, at the age of twenty-five, I was in love. Totally consumed with feeling for him that saturated my whole being. Oblivious to my surroundings, I lived on another plane, where sightings of him consumed me with passion and desire. I had no need of anyone or anything else. He filled my being and transported me to a new world.

Not long after "ev'ry joyous word of love was spoken," Paul came to the convent door and I ran down the stairs to open it. Before either of us knew what was happening, he kissed me, soundly and passionately, then we both stood back and held each other with our eyes and, finally, he gave me something or other for Sister Mary Peter. I said I would see that she got it and turned to go back up the stairs.

He had kissed me. A quiet glow spread throughout my body, and with it a longing never felt before. What was happening?

That night as I lay in my bed remembering his lips on mine something came over me, something physical, warm, and exciting. I took off my nightgown and lay naked on my bed, gently feeling my body with my hands, remembering his long, deep kiss. Slowly, my hand moved to my breasts and down my middle, back and forth across my torso. Slowly my legs separated, and I found the center of my being with my fingers and rubbed slowly while my arms stretched out on the wall and my legs opened wider. My body arched up from the bed, reaching, reaching toward the completion, toward him. Softly rubbing and rubbing until climax and release of energy and love filled my entire being.

Never had I felt like this. Never. Ravaged, I lay naked on the bed conscious of my breathing, conscious of everything, as I had never been before.

The next morning I moved as if in another world, a place apart from the reality of where I was. I did the usual things: Mass, breakfast, school. I saw him the parking lot at lunchtime and our eyes held for a long time. No one seemed to notice anything different about me, but I did. I was different today and would never be the same as I was yesterday. And it was good.

The week passed uneventfully and on Friday evening he somehow managed to meet with me alone in the front parlor. We just sat facing each other and he asked me if I remembered what happened on the stairs. I nodded and he took my hand in his and gently held it. We stood and walked into each other's arms, holding on to each other. Then our heads moved back and then we kissed, long and slow, again and again. Eventually, we separated and he left.

What was I doing? How could I, a nun about to take her final vows, behave this way?

I don't know. To this day I don't know.

The rush of feeling fills me still as I think back to that time, so long ago. I believe with those who really know love can move mountains. My breath comes short to me and my heart pounds a little faster. His lips on mine, his arms around me. Love beyond belief. Sensual but no sex. What could have been…

This is the one Road Not Taken that I've wondered about the most in my life.

In June, just after school got out, my band returned to Holy Family Novitiate in Cumberland, Rhode Island, to prepare to take our final vows. It was so good to see everyone again. Since our first arrival at the novitiate five years ago our numbers had decreased. We went down from thirty-one sisters to twenty-three.

We quickly fell into the routine of charges, prayers, classes, and meditation. Our cells were on the professed side of the novitiate, a real step up for us. I remembered that as novices we had looked forward to the juniors coming to the novitiate to make their final vows. They seemed so mature to us: they seemed to know what they were doing. The beautiful, new chapel lent itself easily to prayer and meditation. We could sit in there for long periods of time and read or just think. I liked saying the Stations of the Cross in the chapel because they were especially beautiful. Sometimes that summer I would do the stations outside, on the hill going from the novitiate to the provincial house. And it was a nice long walk from start to finish.

This summer provided me with the most precious commodity - time. I could be in the chapel and just be alone, just think. So much had happened. I sat in late afternoon, long warm shadows enfolding me. Did I talk to God? Did I pray? Did I really know what I was doing? About to commit myself to poverty, chastity, and obedience for the rest of my life? I knew I was in love with a man, a priest. What kind of a person was I? It is so easy for me to lie to myself. Chastity: I was in love. I wanted Paul sexually. Why couldn't I be honest? Why couldn't I face the truth? I think that my innermost core is wind, not rock. When we spoke to each other, Paul and I tried to convince each other that our relationship was Platonic. That is where I focused my belief. Centuries before, Saint Catherine of Sienna and Saint

Francis of Assisi supposedly had a Platonic relationship. I thought about them a lot that summer. If I had been honest with myself, I would have to admit there was nothing Platonic about Paul and me. The passion of our embraces engulfed every fiber of my being. I was totally in love with him and couldn't wait for his mouth to cover mine and his tongue to meet mine in longing and passion.

That summer at the novitiate was magical. We were the juniors about to take final vows, pledge ourselves irrevocably as Brides of Christ. Sister Mary Peter and I had become very close that year. I think she did not want to believe that I had succumbed to my feelings for Paul. One of the major parts of the ceremony surrounding the taking of our final vows was receiving a ring, symbolizing our marriage to Christ. Inside this ring we could have inscribed a quotation of our choice. I thought long and hard about what I wanted my ring to say and finally decided that I wanted the English translation of Sister Mary Peter's quote. There was no one I loved and admired more as a Sister of St. Edmund than Sister Mary Peter and I thought this gesture would seal our relationship. It is from Paul's epistle to the Romans. "What shall separate me from the love of Christ?" (Romans 8:35) That is one translation. The other is, "Who shall separate me from the love of Christ?" Sister Mary Peter had her inscription in Latin and I decided on the English translation and chose the former, although in retrospect the latter would have been more applicable to me.

Paul came to visit me often that perfect summer. The hill appeared more beautiful than ever and Father Kelly's visits embellished an already wonderful time. Sometimes he came with his friend, Father Schmidt, and sometimes alone. We met in the parlor and he held me with his eyes. I was so in love with him and he with me. We laughed and talked about St. Thomas's, books, our students, everything and anything. He gave some books to me with his hand written loving inscriptions inside. One book in particular became a favorite of mine, <u>Man's Search for Meaning</u>. Paul inscribed the book, "To Irene Joseph, always remember." In it the author, Victor Frankl, writes of his experiences in a concentration camp and how he survived. The main thrust of his premise is that memories will sustain you through anything. And I so totally believe it. The memories of the time Paul and I were in love have sustained me to this day. I remember being breathless, almost unable to speak to him in the parlor that summer. My heart pounded and seemed to close off my vocal cords. I wanted to touch him but didn't. His eyes were full of love and desire but still we did not touch.

I thought about him all the time.

It was so nice having someone from home visiting and updating me about the goings-on in Fall River. Sister Mary Harold was also at the novitiate but he never asked to visit her. He did suggest that I share some of the books with her. I offered to take a walk with him outside, but he said no, that he preferred to visit inside. I realize that he was trying to prevent a scandal about our relationship.

My summer of love. But love of God or love of man? I prayed and meditated and somehow finally convinced myself that love of this man, Paul, personified my love of God. Our love was good, Platonic, holy. I could take a vow of chastity after all.

At last, the day we had been anticipating since before we entered: final vows, August 16, 1967. My family came, Mom, Dad, Anita, Clint, Uncle Eddie, and Agnes. My sponsor, Sister Mary Walter and Sister Mary Peter also came. Once again, we had a beautiful day. The ceremony was long and filled with song (which I lip-synced) and which Father Kelly bellowed out. He came to the ceremony with Father Schmidt.

The ceremony began at two in the afternoon with music, including organ and trumpets. We processed in and went down the steps into the chapel where we sat in the stalls on either side of the marble floor. At one point we again prostrated ourselves on the marble floor with outstretched arms in the form of a cross to symbolize our total submission to Christ. Then we stood and, one by one, approached the altar, where the Bishop placed on our fingers the ring symbolizing our marriage to Christ and pledging our irrevocable fidelity to Him. The inscription on my ring connected me to Sister Mary Peter forever. Glorious music filled the rafters and carried us out of the chapel, where we met our families.

After the ceremony, Paul ran up to me where I was standing with my family and kissed me. My knees melted, I thought I would just crumble up, but I didn't. I'm not sure what my parents thought, me being kissed in public, and especially by a priest. The rest of the day paled in comparison to that moment.

That evening we had a wonderful dinner. It would be the last time we were all together as a band. Newly professed Sisters of St. Edmund about to embark on someone else's goals, someone else's ideas for us. Where would it all lead?

First of all, it led us to The Villa. Most of us would be there. Sister Mary Simon was there from the missions and told wonderful stories of her experiences there. Sister Mary Simon and I had known each other in high school and had been rather close, and, of course, we both majored in math at Salve, so we had spent a lot of time together. She was a VERY SERIOUS NUN. She probably had never broken the Grand Silence in her whole life. At The Villa that summer, I visited with Sister Mary Martha and told her that I thought I was falling in love with Paul Kelly. She warned me to be careful, and distanced herself from me. I was so disappointed by her reaction.

Soon after the ceremony, my parents took Sister Mary Martha and me on a day trip to visit family in Hampton Beach, New Hampshire. It was so much fun. We went swimming in the frigid water and just laughed so much. She had the most wonderful sense of humor. We avoided talking about Father Kelly.

Summer came to an end, and it was back to St. Thomas's and to Paul. I didn't realize the inferno I would meet upon arrival.

CHAPTER 8

Ecstasy and Agony

After I got back to St. Thomas's Convent, Paul stopped by to visit me. It had been such a wonderful summer with him. I was in heaven. We met in the small front parlor and he told me he had applied to graduate school at the University of Illinois at Champaign-Urbana. He was going to pursue a degree in counseling because he felt it would help him be more effective in serving the people of the parish.

The last few weeks before he left, we fell more in love. I didn't think it was possible. He knew how hard it would be for me when he left, so he scheduled it so that he would leave early on the morning of the first day of school. That way I would be busy and, hopefully, distracted. When I came into my classroom, there was a gift from him on my desk with a letter full of love and promise. The gift was a missal with a holy card in it. On the back of the holy card he wrote the words to the Clancy Brothers song he played at his parents home. "It's not the leaving of Liverpool that grieves me, but my darling, when I think of thee." His timing sort of worked. Because I had come to love teaching, I was involved with the students, but still thought about him driving cross-country.

Once he arrived at the University of Illinois, our letter writing began. Every day, right after school, I would go straight to the mailbox just inside the back hall. If there were a letter from him, I would hug it and put it in my pocket to be read later. I wanted to cherish it as long as I could. None of these letters have been saved. I'm sorry I didn't save them. But I can remember them. I see his handwriting now on the envelopes. In one of the letters he told me about his brother and his family, who were also in Champaign at the time. Paul wrote that he had stopped by to visit Dan and his wife and found them relaxing together in front of the fire. He wrote that seeing them so close made him feel lonely for me.

In another one he wrote, "I'm lying in bed writing to you and wishing you were here with me." What kept me from going? Why didn't I just leave the convent then and go to him, embrace him and spend the rest of my life with him? I had just taken final vows to remain a virgin, married to Christ. Conflict began to build in me about my decision. A germ of questioning came into my heart, but it was small.

I was so in love. My body was in a constant state of arousal, something I had never felt before falling in love with Paul.

In class, I would be teaching and think of him. One day it began snowing and it was as if I saw snow for the first time ever in my life. What joy in my heart! I could feel his arms around me, holding me, embracing me. There is a song in "The Music Man" that expresses what I felt so much better than I can:

There were bells on a hill
But I never heard them ringing
No, I never heard them at all
Till there was you
There were birds in the sky
But I never saw them winging
No, I never saw them at all
Till there was you
Then there was music and wonderful roses
They tell me in sweet fragrant meadows
Of dawn and dew
There was love all around
But I never heard it singing
No, I never heard it at all
Till there was you
Then there was music and wonderful roses
They tell me in sweet fragrant meadows

Joan Fox

Of dawn and dew
There was love all around
But I never heard it singing
No, I never heard it at all
Till there was you
Till there was you

(From "The Music Man", book, music, and lyrics by Meredith Wilson)

After he left for Illinois, I threw myself into teaching. I so loved it. The kids were just great. There is nothing like working with a group of preadolescents to challenge and uplift you. No two days – even hours - are ever the same.

Paul came home for winter break in early December and I couldn't wait to see him alone. At last, he came to the convent and we met in the parlor. We slowly moved into each other's arms, held each other, and our lips met. After a while we sat across from each other and he gave me Christmas gifts he had brought from the University of Illinois. One was a huge university mug; it's actually the only one of the gifts I remember. I had it on my desk in my cell for ages. He began to tell me all about his life at the university: his classes, the people he met, and happiness at being home, here with me. One of his classes required that he administer a personality test and he asked me if I would be willing to participate for him. And I said yes, of course. So we arranged for another meeting and we sat down to do the test. He recorded the session so he would be able to write the paper when he got back to Illinois. Later he told me that when his professor heard the tape, she could tell that there was real love between us, just from the sound of our voices.

Paul invited Sister Mary Brendan and me to go with him to La Salette Shrine in Attleboro, Massachusetts, to see the Christmas lights. He was taking his nephews and niece, ages three to eight, and we would help him with the children. It was like a date for me. He picked us up and Sister Mary Brendan sat in the back with the boys and I sat in the front with Ed and his niece.

Before I knew it his hand reached across her and held mine. He drove all the way with one hand on the wheel and the other holding mine. I was in heaven. His intimate touch filled me with softness and a yearning for more.

Once we were there, we walked around the shrine admiring the lights and then had supper in the cafeteria. It was like being a family: mom, dad, the kids, and grandma. I was in heaven. His niece, Ann, had to go to the bathroom so I took her. She was a pistol. After she washed her hands, I wanted to get back to Paul but she kept pushing the hand dryer. I literally had to drag her back to the table. We finally got back in the car and drove home, Paul and I holding hands again, every now and then gently squeezing each other's hands. The children were falling asleep. When we arrived at the convent, he held the door open for me and helped me out of the car. Our eyes met, held and the promise of more in them kept me going. It was a magical night.

We saw each other alone once more on the night before he left. Our embraces long and slow filled me with love and desire. I wanted him so much, in every way. His kisses were deep and hungry; our tongues sought each other, his eyes full of love and desire. His hand slipped down to my waist and then upward to my breast. Gently he touched me everywhere and I felt it in my innermost being. We moved to the couch and held each other exploring our bodies, desire growing rapidly. My body began a rhythmic movement in tune with his, slowly at first, gradually with more passion. He slipped his fingers between my legs and gently rubbed back and forth, round and round. I throbbed and could barely wait for him to enter me. We exploded with passion. Afterward, we lay in each other's arms kissing and feeling our bodies against one another. I have never been so completely happy.

The next morning he left.

Tension built in the convent over Christmas break. The nuns were really upset that I was spending so much time with Paul. Sister Mary Peter was noticeably cold, so unlike her. What could she do? Here was a young nun obviously involved with a priest and totally unwilling to give up the relationship.

Joan Fox

They attacked my teaching. Sister Mary Rose, Assistant Superintendent of Schools, came to my classroom early in February, soon after Paul returned to Illinois, for my annual evaluation and observed me in my classroom. Her scathing criticism cut me to the core. According to her, I did nothing right in the classroom. On my desk was a set of essays, which I had graded. She went through them with a fine toothcomb and pointed out every mistake I had made, said I should have done a much better job with them. Teaching was my life and I put everything I had into it and that scathing criticism nearly destroyed me. I didn't think I would ever recover. I was in tears afterward, totally devastated, and went to Sister Mary Peter for solace. None there. How unfair of them to tear apart my teaching because they thought my relationship with Paul was wrong. Why not just say that and be done with it? I still feel the pain I felt then from the attack on my teaching. How mean and cruel it was, how misdirected.

I eagerly awaited the first letter from Paul and was not disappointed. It was filled with memories of our time together at Christmas and reading it thrilled me. I wished he were with me. I responded quickly and lovingly. Winter sparkled around me and filled me with anticipation of being with him again. I knew it wouldn't be until spring break, but that was okay. It took longer than usual for him to write back and I began to wonder what was happening. Maybe he was busy with classes. Still no letter. Then, when it finally arrived, the tone was different. By now it was the middle of February. I wrote back that I missed him and could feel his arms around me and his lips on mine. I eagerly awaited his response. He never replied. I thought it was because he was busy with classes and would be home soon for spring break in March.

I began to count the days until his arrival. At last I saw his car in the parking lot and hoped he would be here to see me. It was several days after his arrival that he came at last to the convent. We met in the parlor, where I stepped into his arms only to feel him stiffen and slowly step back from me.

"I have something to tell you, Irene Joseph." We sat down across from each other and his eyes held mine, but we didn't touch. He began:

80

"These last few months have been difficult for me. I have always said that if our friendship interfered with our religious life, it should end. After Christmas vacation, a woman (another nun, now ex-nun) came to see me in Champaign. You may have met her. She was a Sacred Heart nun here in Fall River. We began to see each other fairly often and one thing led to another. I have decided to leave the priesthood and when the dispensation comes through, I will marry her. We are expecting a baby. It will be very difficult for me in the near future. I have no idea if I will be welcomed back by my family. I need your friendship and support now more than ever."

If I were a great writer, I could put into words what I felt then, but I cannot. Cold. I remember feeling very cold, empty, and stiff. My entire being disappeared. I could have crumbled into a pile of dust – dust thou art and unto dust thou shalt return. I was nothing. My heart stopped. My soul faded away. Who was I? What had happened? How could this have happened? I loved him so. And he had loved me. Here, before me, his eyes on mine. I stood and turned away.

"I hope you can understand," he pled.

"I can't. Please go."

"Irene Joseph, please."

"Leave, leave now."

He left. He was gone from me.

I dragged myself upstairs to my cell, too stunned to even cry or yell or scream. There was nothing of me to react. I lay on the bed, unable to move.

I was empty. I had no desire to live. How could I go on? The next morning I got up, went to school, ate, pretended to pray, went to bed, pretended to be alive. I died a little every moment. We had shared so many moments together. My mind kept questioning: Does he think about our time together the intimate moments, the touches, the words we spoke to each other, the passion? Will he come to see me one more time before he leaves and hold me one more time? Will he regret his choice? My heart thuds. Will I ever get over this? I see him at Mass and can't believe that he loved me. I feel his hands on me, feel him inside me, and remember. I wonder if he does, too. I think of him constantly. He has someone else now, but he can't just obliterate what we had. How long will he remember me? He took me to the stars. I will always have him within me. Nothing can change that. And I was in him. The total physical attraction we had for each other was incredible. I anticipated his touch, his letters, his voice, and his eyes. He had loved me and I loved him. Someone asked me the other day, over forty years later, what was the happiest time of my life, and, without a moment's hesitation, I said when I was in love with Paul Kelly and he was in love with me. Nothing compares to that.

I taught the next day and the next day and the next day and so on. Paul tried to talk to me but I would have none of it. There was nothing left of me to talk to. Finally, he left for Illinois and I began to breathe again. And I began to think about the situation. My heart was his and always would be. I knew that. And now, over forty years later, it still is. I decided that he did not know how much I was in love with him so I wrote to him and told him that I loved him as a wife loves her husband.

His response was quick and somewhat emotional, for himself, not me.

> *May 14, 1968*
> *Dear Irene Joseph,*
> *I really do not know what to say because I feel so badly. I have considered marriage for a very long time and this consideration had been the great cross of my past life. I tried to put it away from my mind and heart, but I never could. Then I came to love you because you were the only possible way of my really loving someone without the love demanding marital union. My love for you was and is sincere, but I came to realize that the love I truly was seeking was the love of a wife.*
>
> *Now, it seems, I have done to you what I so feared all along – hurt you. So often I said if our love ever led to anything that caused hurt or distraction from work, or anything else, that was a sign of too deep an emotional involvement, it would have to cease.*

The bishop has forwarded my papers to Rome and now I wait to be dispensed. Then I will marry.

I don't know when or if I will ever be free to come home again or if I'll be received if I do come home. Should I ever come home, I would want to see you, if possible not with the pain that now is between us.

Irene Joseph, I am troubled and almost alone without almost anyone who cares. I am deeply sorry for the hurt I have caused you. I know it will go away. When it does, I pray you will not remember me as one who brought you darkness, but hopefully, as one who loved you and still does.

Paul

I never responded.

By now it was near the end of spring. I went through the motions of teaching. The nuns noticed that his picture was gone from my desk and that no letters were arriving from him. He maintained correspondence with Sister Mary Brendan and in one of his letters to her he asked her to get me to burn the letters he had written to me. And I did. She walked with me down to the basement to the burner and into the fire they went. I wish I hadn't done that.

Many years later, we corresponded once or twice and I still have those letters. He settled in Maryland with his wife and family. When my daughter went to college in a town not far from where he lived, I called him from the motel room where I stayed while visiting her. We talked for a while: I can't remember what we said, except that he admitted that he still remembered. And so do I. It was the last time we spoke. He died three years later.

Falling in love and having that love returned is the essence of living. How fortunate I was to have had that. To this day I wonder what it would be like to have followed him to Illinois. Maybe it's better just to imagine.

Do I have regrets? I guess I do. I wish I had gone to him. She had the courage to go to him. Why didn't I?

Gradually, I began to notice that the sun still came out, life went on. That was the most surprising thing for me. It's sort of like when someone dies whom you loved. Your world seems to end but the rest of the world doesn't realize that everything should stop because you are in such pain. It seems unreal that people go to work, cook, shop, eat, and sleep even though your beloved has died. How can that be? I felt that way every day that spring. My heart weighed a ton: it dragged me down. The other nuns in the convent noticed that I put his picture face down on my desk. I couldn't bear to look at him.

It was truly over. For him, but not for me. I loved him still.

But life must go on and, very slowly, I began to think that maybe I could live and maybe even find love again. Nothing compared to the way I felt when I was with Paul. I felt whole, complete, and so alive! I began to think about leaving the convent. I wondered if I could find love again.

To make a decision like this, I needed time and distance from my present emotional state. Once again, logic took over and, rather than leave religious life right away, I decided to stay in the convent at least one more year to see if my feelings changed.

Just after I made this decision, on June 6, 1968, instead of the usual "Lord Jesus preserve us in peace," Sister Marie Luke banged on our cell doors crying that Bobby Kennedy had been shot. His Presidential campaign ended with the assassin's bullet. I had entered the convent at the beginning of JFK's campaign, so filled with hope. Another assassin had taken him down. Where would it all end?

During the summer of 1968, I was transferred from St. Thomas's to St. Matthew's Convent in Warwick, Rhode Island. My last year in the convent was about to begin.

CHAPTER NINE

Recovery

I arrived at St. Matthew's in August of 1968, fully realizing that it would probably be my last year in the convent. My heart had been torn apart by the love I had for Paul. I was still dazed.

Saying goodbye to Sister Mary Peter was especially hard for me. I loved her and, to say the least, had not been the best of nuns for her. I told her my plan was to spend the upcoming year thinking about my future in the convent and she thought I was wise to think things through. What had I unknowingly done to her? Was I black mark on her "career" in religious life? Yes, there are careers in the convent. Politics is everywhere. She was oblivious to it and simply stove to be the best possible sister she could be. We promised to keep in touch and we did. Her support for me once again was invaluable.

Gradually, I fell into the routine at St. Matthew's. The superior there, Sister Mary Andrew, had a reputation for being rather lax, which worked out well for me. Sister Mariam Timothy and Sister Jane Mary were young nuns and we got to be close friends. One of my all time favorite nuns was Sister Mary Kenneth, who taught third grade at St. Matthew's. Sister Mary Kenneth was very short and a little bent over besides. She had a round, pink face with no wrinkles - no wrinkles - and she must have been at least seventy-nine years old. It's that Irish complexion, for she was also from the old sod. Remember Sister Mary Jude, the cook at St. Thomas's? Sister Mary Kenneth reminded me of her. She was a happy, warm, loving nun, who cheerfully went about her duties day after day. I loved talking with her because I always felt better afterward. Sister Mary Kenneth made me feel good inside. If anyone is in heaven, she is, and I hope she knows how much she meant to me. Once it became known that I was leaving, she was wonderful. She understood. And that meant so much to me.

It was nice being closer to my parents. I saw them pretty often now. Religious life had changed so much since I entered the convent and changed for the better, because the nuns were allowed to have relationships with their families and friends. My Mom and Dad were even allowed to have a formal portrait taken of me at Lorings Studio in Providence. I actually still have it, covered as it is now with my wedding portrait. One day, in late fall, I was at my parent's home for dinner and I told them I was thinking about leaving religious life. My Mother didn't say much and neither did my Dad but I felt that they were okay with the idea. They wanted to know what made me consider this after all this time. I know I didn't tell them that I had fallen in love. I can't remember what I said. My parents were there for me in so many ways.

Once school started, my mind was occupied with teaching. I was assigned to teach eighth grade everything and fourth grade science. That was so bad because the students knew more than I did in science. The seventh grade teacher was Elaine Ivarone, a gorgeous young woman who became a dear friend. She would be a bridesmaid at my wedding less than two years later. We had so much fun teaching together. Her specialty was English so we decided to departmentalize: she would teach English to seventh and eighth graders and I would teach math. Her husband, Charlie, taught at a nearby public middle school. He was quite handsome and drove a brand new mustang, red. They were living in the fast lane.

My classroom lined up with the flight path for Theodore Francis Greene Airport. The first time I realized this, I was in the middle of an algebra class. "If a plane leaves city A flying at a speed of 600 mph…" I looked out the window and stood face to face with a Boeing 747 heading straight for my classroom and me. I think if I were outside, I could have touched the belly of the plane. I was so scared. Arriving planes were never as bad as takeoffs because takeoffs headed directly for me in my class-room. And the sound was nothing to sneeze at, either. My hear-ing is impaired as a result of that experience. What did you say?

After I settled in at school and in the convent, I started to think about my future. Should I stay in the convent or should I leave? It was a complicated decision to make. I had taken final vows, wore the ring of a Bride of Christ, committed myself for life to God. Why did I want to leave the convent? To be hon-est, I wanted to find love again. I did pray about it but it didn't help. So I began to ask myself, "Why did I enter the convent in the first place?" To do something worthwhile with my life. But everything was different now. I had fallen in love. Religious life was different from what it was when I entered. I considered the possibility that I could live a good life without being a nun. Besides, my standard of living in the convent in Warwick was higher than that of the people I had worked with in Fall River. It seemed unfair that I should be better off as a nun, with a vow of poverty, than the parishioners in Fall River. But this fact only made it a little easier to leave the convent and to be sure my reason was not altruistic at all. I wanted to find human, physical love.

Gradually, I recognized that, in truth, I was not really a nun anymore. I would leave the convent. To that end, I sought out a spiritual advisor who would recommend to the Congregation of Religious Life in Rome that I should be dispensed from my vows. After asking several friends for suggestions of a spiritual advisor, I went to Father Mort, who also just happened to be drop-dead gorgeous. Spiritual guidance was a process I had to go through in order to be released from my vows. When he asked me why I wanted to leave the convent, I said it was because I wanted to find a love like the one I had with Paul. I spoke with candidly about the relationship that Paul and I had. I wanted to find that again. Does anyone find another first love? Father Mort saw clearly that I was no longer a nun in my heart and helped the process along for me.

Soon after I arrived at St. Matthew's, Father Philip Mahoney, the priest from Somerset, came to visit me. We had been writing to each other for some time. Although he knew Paul from Fall River, neither of us ever mentioned him. I remembered how Father Mahoney used to bring me little gifts at St. Thomas's. He was so handsome and so attentive. Who knows what the nuns at St. Matthew's thought about him visiting me? By that time, we could wear secular clothes, so I dressed for the occasion and met him in the parlor. ("Come into my parlor," said the spider to the fly.) I don't remember how we arranged it, but we managed to leave and went with a friend of his who was driving a pick up truck. We all sat in the front and went to a place where he could get a drink. Phil and I stayed in the truck and necked. Most fun than I'd had in a while, a really long while. He really wanted me and it was great. All too soon, his friend came back and they dropped me off at the convent.

The next morning, Sister Mariam Timothy asked me if I knew Phil was coming before he showed up. I said no. I lied. I was still keeping secret the fact that I intended to leave the convent at the end of the year. However, not long after that, I did tell her and Sister Jane Mary my plan to leave. They weren't surprised.

Now that the decision had been made, I had to make plans for the next step in my life. I would need to get a job in order to support myself. So I started to apply to graduate schools, with the goal of getting a master's degree in counseling and a job as a guidance counselor in a public school. I applied to graduate schools on the west coast, University of Minnesota, and the University of Connecticut. I was also taking some grad courses at Rhode Island College, where one of my professors was Myron Lieberman, whom I loved. He was from Minnesota and wrote a wonderful recommendation for me. Unfortunately, I didn't get accepted at the University of Minnesota, but did get accepted everywhere else. I finally decided on the University of Connecticut because it was close to my parents, but not too close.

Next, I had to find a job close to the university. As luck would have it, the town of Mansfield, Connecticut, was in the process of building a new middle school and was hiring new staff. They needed a math teacher, so I applied.

88

They invited me for an interview, and on a day during my April vacation, my parents drove me to Mansfield. We had lunch at Eaton Farms, on Route 195, and then drove over to Buchanan School, where the superintendent had his office. My parents waited in the car while I went in. Of course, I still wore my nun's habit but I was not prepared for the reaction as I entered the large room where the support personnel worked. Every head in the place turned to look at me. Suddenly, it was very quiet. Adele McGann, the superintendent's secretary, asked if she could help me and I said I was here for an interview with Dr. Norman Lovett. She said he was expecting me and would see me momentarily. Frank Crowley, the newly hired principal, was meeting with Dr. Lovett. The door opened and they invited me in. The interview went well. Toward the end of the interview, Dr. Lovett asked me how much time I spent teaching religion in my present position and I said one half hour a day. He was looking to cut back on the credit he would give me for my experience, but he gave me the full five years. The next question was about my availability for the upcoming summer. The new Mansfield Middle School wanted to incorporate Illinois Math into the program and needed faculty to be trained. A National Science Foundation institute was being offered at The University of Connecticut in the summer. The institute would provide me with housing, pay me for attending, and pay the cost of the classes. I said yes, I would be able to do it. Actually, it was perfect for me since I had no other income and no place to live. A few weeks later they wrote and told me I had the job. It turned out to be one of the most fulfilling experiences of my life. And, I would finally be a real college girl, after all.

I actually had to write to the Pope to request a dispensation, which I did, and it eventually came in the mail. The entire document was written in Latin, so I have no idea what it said, but I left anyway, in June of 1969, after spending almost ten years of my life in the convent.

I remember the day fairly well. It was a Sunday, just after my eighth graders graduated from St. Matthew's. I said good-bye to them and their parents, came back to the convent, and went

Joan Fox

into the parlor. I don't remember any of the sisters being there to say good-bye to me. I wonder where they were? I remember being alone in the room with lines of light filtering through the Venetian blinds. Slowly, I began to take off my habit, and with it a life that would be no more, peeled away. First, the veil, followed by the habit. Shoes and stockings were next. My parents had brought clothes for me to wear home and I put them on. The only thing left was my ring. I looked at it for a long time before taking it off my finger and placing it on my habit. I straightened out the pile, turned, and left.

CPSIA information can be obtained at www.ICGtesting.com
Printed in the USA
BVOW03s2152220713

326677BV00001B/13/P